Z.A.P., ZOE,
AND THE MUSKETEERS

ATHENA V. LORD

Z.A.P., ZOE, AND THE MUSKETEERS

MACMILLAN PUBLISHING COMPANY
New York
MAXWELL MACMILLAN CANADA
Toronto
MAXWELL MACMILLAN INTERNATIONAL
New York   Oxford   Singapore   Sydney

I wish to thank the following who added and confirmed the accuracy of historical details: Kay Stevens and Malcolm Horton, officers of the Hudson Valley Chapter of the Steamship Historical Society of America, J. Cameron and Patricia Brown, Franklin Myers, and the Rev. Father Patric Legato.

Macmillan Publishing Company is part of the Maxwell Communication Group of Companies.
Macmillan Publishing Company
866 Third Avenue, New York, NY 10022
Maxwell Macmillan Canada, Inc.
1200 Eglinton Avenue East, Suite 200, Don Mills, Ontario M3C 3N1
First Edition
Printed in the United States of America

1   3   5   7   9   10   8   6   4   2

The text of this book is set in 12 pt. Century Schoolbook.

Library of Congress Cataloging-in-Publication Data
Lord, Athena V.
Z.A.P., Zoe, and the musketeers / by Athena V. Lord. —
1st ed.
p.   cm.
Summary: Zach, his little sister Zoe, and their friends try to create an exciting summer in Albany, New York, in the early 1940s.
ISBN 0-02-759561-7
[1. Brothers and sisters—Fiction. 2. Friendship—Fiction. 3. Greek Americans—Fiction.] I. Title. II. Title: Zap, Zoe, and the musketeers.
PZ7.L8769Zap   1992   [Fic]—dc20   91-31049

To P.A.L.
who has been a true pal for more years
and in more ways than I can count.

Contents

1
The New Coach

"Zach, if you could be anything at all . . ."

Zoe was so close her voice buzzed in my ear like a giant horsefly. She stood on an overturned pail waiting for me to hand her some more spoons.

If I could be anything at all . . .

How did Zoe know I've been thinking of exactly that? The last time I took a bath, I found these new little hairs growing in a line down to my belly button. A discovery like that starts you thinking seriously about growing up. Maybe I'll join the army and become a tank commander like General George Patton. Or I wouldn't mind being Bob Hope. His movies make everybody laugh.

Even if I'm not sure what I want to be, I know one thing: I wouldn't pick working in the kitchen of our family's luncheonette in Albany, New York. Not this summer of 1941, not any summer of my life. I stepped back from the sink to lean out and look again at the big wall clock in the front of our store. A quarter to two. The sooner the hands on that clock moved, the sooner I could escape and meet my friends.

My friends and I, we like to stick together. Though to be honest, I'm not too keen about Wylie Bowen, a kid who's here visiting his aunt this summer. Wylie is older—fourteen, maybe even fifteen years old, and sometimes he comes up with strange ideas of things to do. I don't exactly trust him, I guess.

"Zachary Athanasius Poulos, you're not listening to me."

"Zoe, for what you're saying, I'm listening enough."

I feel like all the summers of my life have been filled with listening to and keeping an eye on my peanut-sized sister Zoe, who's going on six. Between the two jobs—minding Zoe, and working in the store—it's hard to find free time for my friends.

It can be done. I know, because I use a lot of brain power setting up ways to do it. For instance, I told Zoe that working makes you grow taller. Naturally, she begged to be allowed to help. Out of the goodness of my heart I let her dry the silverware, and now I get to leave the store by two.

"Zach, if you could be anything, anything at all *except* a human bean, what would you pick?"

Seven minutes left till quitting time.

Going back to Zoe's question, I gave it two seconds

of thought. "What would I be *except* a human being? That's easy. God."

Zoe's thick black eyebrows climbed high in surprise and disappeared under her bangs. Her round black-olive eyes grew rounder still and her mouth made a pink O.

"Oooh. What you said!"

"You asked and I gave you an answer, an honest answer," I said, feeling kind of cross. Mama always tells us to aim high in life, and that's become one of my rules.

Zoe's eyes rolled up to the ceiling. "Pick something else. Pick to be a butterfly or a tree or something."

"No, Zoe. I said God and I mean G—"

"Noooo," Zoe wailed.

She did more than that. She jumped from the pail onto me, clapped her hands across my mouth, and knocked us both down.

Have I mentioned that taking care of Zoe is often dangerous to your health? That kid can go from being a pest to a menace faster than a speeding bullet.

"You can't want that," she cried. "God will punish you for wanting to push Him out. Remember the thunderbolts?"

Oops, now I got it. She had mixed up the Bible God with the Greek gods in the old myths. In those the gods battle each other and punish anybody who tries to steal their powers. We've been reading myths since we were little because our family came from Greece. Matter of fact, all our relatives including *yiayia*, Mama's mother, still live there in a village called Vlasti.

"Off, kid, before I suffocate." She was sitting on my chest, trying to protect me from those jealous gods, I guess.

"Zoe, you heard me but you weren't listening. I said I would *be* him, not push him out of his place."

She looked doubtful, but at least she moved off and I got up. Thanks to Zoe's loving and worrying about me, it was past two. Quickly I untied my white waiter's apron. I started for the screen door so fast you'd think those old gods really were throwing thunderbolts at me.

"*Zaharia* . . ."

Mama's voice was calling me in Greek. I didn't answer. After all, by the clock, I was supposed to be off duty.

Mama, who had been out back in the garden, poked her head from behind the partition separating the kitchen and the customers in front. She said, "*Zaharia*, the knife grinder is outside. I can hear the sharpening wheel. Carry these knives out to him. *Now*."

You can't really take your own mother to court,

but I bet Mama is violating the child labor laws with all the work she keeps giving me. I went back for the handful of knives that she had wrapped in a dish towel and crossed the street to the little triangle of a park that separates Central and Washington Avenues.

Otto, the grinder man, had set up his wheel by the horse watering trough at the end point. Ahead of me in line was the Armenian butcher from the corner meat market. Just my luck. He had a whole apron full of choppers and cleavers to be sharpened. Adding to my bad luck Zoe had hurried across to the park behind me. She joined the bunch of kids watching the sparks fly as the grinding wheel turned.

"Let me hold a knife, too, Zach," she asked. "It's no fair you have them all. I'm big enough to do this job, Zachary."

My uh-uh didn't stop her.

"Why-can't-I, why-can't-I?" she sing-songed along with the hum of the wheel.

"Because," I snapped. She knows as well as I that knives and matches are two things Mama is strict about.

"Bossy Zach, you always grab the fun jobs for yourself," Zoe grumbled. "It's my store, too, 'n' they're my knives, too."

Her argument about the store and knives wasn't

worth answering. "I only take matters into my own hands when they're *safer* there," I pointed out, stressing the word safer.

"Sh-she can carry m-mine," said a man at the head of the line whose knife was just finished. It was the youngish man we call Shaky John. He has something wrong with him. When he walks, he shuffles, his head bobs up and down, and he can't talk well. He doesn't go to work anywhere. Mostly he sits on a bench in Washington Park or in our little park.

"Re-tard. Moron," said a voice just loud enough to be heard. It came from the edge of the crowd where Wylie Bowen was standing.

Shaky John's cheeks turned a bright red as he said to me, "It's in a case so—so it's safe. I'm sit-sitting there." He nodded toward a nearby bench— or tried to, but his head swung wildly out of control. Some kids snickered.

Zoe didn't notice, and she didn't wait. She took the case from Shaky John and proudly led the way to the bench. When she came back, she asked in a clear, carrying voice, "Zachary, why does Shaky John shake like that?"

"Why don't you ask Shaky himself?" teased Mousie Mertz, making his usual face. His nose twitches every time he says something.

"Don't encourage her," I said.

"People like that are good for nothing and

shouldn't be taking up space on public property."
It sounded like Wylie talking again.

I heard some "Yeahs" of agreement. I have to say
I don't like to share a bench with Shaky John,
either. Besides stuttering, sometimes he sprays
when he talks. Still, I don't think it's Wylie's or my
business to decide who can sit where in a city park.

"Maybe we oughtta do something about it," said
Wylie.

I surprised myself with what I said next. I announced loudly, "You can do what you want, but
I'm not sticking around. I'm going on an expedition,
a real adventure."

"Include me in," said Abe Zalkin, who'd just
joined us.

"Me, too, but I have to be back by suppertime.
Where you going?" Patty Aylward asked.

Patty's only a girl, but next to Abe, she's my best
friend. Her middle name is Zelda and Abe's middle
name is Pincus, so we all share the initials Z, A,
and P. Abe wants to send our names to *Ripley's
Believe It or Not*. Chances are that no other neighborhood in the world has three, I mean four, kids
with that combination. Zoe's middle name is Athanasius, like mine, so we have to include her. We call
ourselves the Four Musketeers after the characters
in the adventure book. We have the same motto,
too: All for one, and one for all.

Anyway, the fact is that I didn't have any adventure in mind at all. I only wanted to get us off the subject of Shaky John, but my tongue had gone faster than my brain. And now all the kids started asking for details and to be included.

I waved them off, saying, "I'll let you know."

Abe and Patty kept me company while I took the knives back to the store. Abe said it would be easier to go to the moon than to find an adventure in Albany, New York. He's almost thirteen like me, but he's got more world experience. The Zalkins are refugees who escaped from the Nazis in Austria. Already Abe has traveled across two oceans from Europe to Cuba and then from Cuba to the U.S.

"If we had a couple of dollars, we could at least take the bus to Mid-City Park. That pool is open already," Abe suggested.

"I have only a quarter. And I'd need to pay Zoe's way, too," I pointed out. "So nix on Mid-City."

Patty asked, "How about the library? We could look through the stereopticon."

I made a face. Every chance she gets, Zoe drags me into helping her look at those cards that slip into a viewer and turn into three-dimensional scenes.

"You could call it a sight-seeing expedition because we'd be looking at the Grand Canyon and Niagara Falls," Abe argued.

"Everybody's seen every card in the box a zillion times. No tourist in real life goes to look at the same sight over and over," I answered. "But, hey, I think I have an idea."

"Does it hurt much?" Abe asked sympathetically.

I gave him a friendly chop on the arm and said, "Listen, what I have in mind is perfect: free and not too many kids have been there."

I knew I was right. Nobody ever pays attention to what's in his own city. It's only if you travel someplace else that you go sight-seeing.

After rounding up all the kids and walking a short way down Washington Avenue, I called a halt. The expression on their faces was worth seeing. You never saw such confused-looking people.

"This is our adventure? A two-block walk?" Mousie asked, his voice squeaking in disbelief.

"Follow Zach or shut up and go home," Abe directed in that bossy way of his. "You have to trust the leader."

"That's called the Institute of History and Art," I said waving at a gray stone building set back from the street. It looks like a rich man's house with a big green lawn in front.

Louie the Lip, who mostly keeps his mouth shut as in "button your lip," spoke up. "I've heard of it. What's it got to do with us?"

"You've been living here all your life, right? Well, it's past time we, the inhabitants of this capital city, checked out what's in the place and what kind of shape it's in."

17

On account of Albany being the capital of New York State, we have more than one museum here. The librarian, who's always trying to educate me, told me about this one. I led the eight of us up the steps and through heavy double doors.

"Zach, if it costs to get in, I don't have any money," Patty whispered.

The high ceiling and marble floors in this place made you want to whisper. "I told you. It's public so it's free," I said, forcing my voice to stay at regular volume.

On both sides of the hall, stairs curved down out of sight. Louie was stretching his neck to look up at the walls where huge, dark paintings of people in George Washington-style clothes hung. On a pedestal by the door was a white marble head. Tiny Carlson, who's bigger than any of us, stood eye to eye with the long-nosed statue. He studied it and said, "Zach, this reminds me too much of school."

"For crying out loud, we're barely in the door. You're not giving this place a chance," I said, annoyed.

Down the wide hall, a uniformed guard made the rounds of the rooms off the hall. I recognized him as a customer of ours, the one Zoe nicknamed Grumpy because he's always complaining.

Just to be on the safe side, I shoved some of the kids toward the stairs and said, "Let's start from the bottom up."

Abe, who's no dummy, grabbed Zoe by the hand, and the two of them were first to clatter down the stairs. The basement was even more hushed than the upstairs and was kind of dim. Glass cases with baskets and old pots lined the walls. Folding chairs set up in rows faced a big grand piano.

"Not too much in the way of adventure here," Abe observed.

Zoe eyed the piano. I knew what was coming next, so I said to her, "No, you can't play the piano. Go read the labels on the cases."

Zoe has been reading both Greek and English since before she started kindergarten. I taught her how because it helped to keep her out of my hair.

"Zach, I can't read these. Too hard," she complained.

I heard her, but I didn't see her in the room where we were still standing. "Where did you get to now?" I asked. "Come back here."

"No, you come here. Why is this statue lying down in the box, Zach? Why does it say over 2,000 years?"

I spotted Zoe in an alcove on the right. She had her nose pressed to the glass of a large, long case set low on the floor. I joined her and could hardly believe it when I looked down into the case. Then I read the label.

"Abe, Patty, you guys, come get a load of what Zoe found. He's a real human being. Can you believe he was alive once?"

We stood in total silence looking at a dark, wrapped-up genuine Egyptian mummy. You can't help but have respect for something that old.

"Oh, Zach, they didn't finish wrapping this one up," said Zoe, who had drifted over to the glass case on the opposite wall. Her voice shook as she spoke.

Louie the Lip, who had followed Zoe, practically screeched, "The whole skull is here. Look at those empty eye sockets."

Everybody moved over to get a good look at this new mummy whose bones looked like black iron.

"Imagine those bony fingers reaching for your neck," Abe added, and stretched out his hands toward Patty. She gave a little yelp as she batted them down.

"I wonder if he gets up and walks in the night," I said.

Zoe backed away. "Let's go home, Zachary. I wanna get out of here." She clutched my hand with fingers almost as iron-hard as the mummy's looked to be.

"Zoe, don't be a wet blanket. Go back by the piano if you don't like it here," I said, shaking her hand free from mine.

"If we had a movie camera, we could make a great film here," said Tiny Carlson, eyeing the half-wrapped mummy.

"We gotta go home, Zachary," Zoe's voice rose in a loud wail.

"You mean, *you* want to go home," I answered.

Changing tactics, Zoe turned to Abe. "There's Nazis here, Abe. We have to go this second."

I have to give Zoe credit for being one smart cookie. She knows how much Abe hates the Nazis. "Ignore her and she'll calm down," I said.

Famous last words. I should know better than anyone how stubborn Zoe can be. She beat a hasty retreat out of the alcove all right. But she headed straight to the piano and hit the black and white keys with both fists. The banging, clanging noise was enough to bring both mummies back from the dead.

The racket got everybody's attention, and Zoe pointed wordlessly at a case on the wall. It was all little stones, set in what's called a mosaic. The design they made was a swastika!

"Holy Nellie," shouted Tiny, pointing to the left-hand staircase. Two men in gray green uniforms pounded down the stairs toward us.

"Beat it," I yelled, grabbing Zoe and dragging her like a rag doll up the right-hand staircase. Behind me I heard more crashing and banging. The folding chairs were being knocked down by the rush of kids. We were out and across the street before I looked back again.

Three guards stood in the doorway, waving their fists at us. Grumpy was yelling, "You hoodlums don't belong in here. Don't come in ever again."

21

"Whew! Good thing those guys are old like the stuff in the museum and can't run very fast," Abe observed. We both laughed as we turned to head back to the little park.

"How can you laugh?" asked Mousie Mertz. "Shouldn't we tell somebody about those Nazis?" When God passed out brains, Mousie must have been hiding behind the door.

Abe gave Mousie a pitying look. "Since when did you think the Nazis had occupied the U.S.A.? That mosaic is an old Roman thing from somebody's house. The label said the guy was called Hadrian."

I like reading about the old Romans and Greeks. It doesn't seem fair somehow that we got chased away from the museum. If only Zoe hadn't panicked. . . .

I didn't know how much worse things could get until the next afternoon. All the kids sat on the steps of the Spanish-American War monument at the far end of the park, waiting. Waiting for me to produce another treat. In fact, they acted like I owed it to them.

Zoe didn't help matters any when she asked, "Zach, if we don't belong in the museum, where can we go? What can we do?"

"C'mon, Zach. You're falling down on the job," said Louie impatiently.

"What job? Do you think I'm the counselor whose

job it is to keep all you little campers happy?" I asked, glaring at them.

"When I heard your nickname was ZAP, I thought it'd be exciting around there this summer," drawled Wylie Bowen. "If you want us to play follow the leader with you, you better start zapping somebody or something. Or else . . ."

I can't figure out how he managed to make it a sneer and a threat both at the same time. "I never claimed to be Superman, and I never asked you to follow me. You're the ones who begged yesterday to come along. What you're talking about is showing off, and I hate show-offs," I answered. In any contest for ungrateful people, my friends would take first prize, I decided.

Abe hooted. "Don't try to say you don't like bossing everybody around."

Abe's remark was the straw that broke my camel's back—or my patience, I mean. Maybe I do like to kind of plan and take charge of things. That doesn't mean I'm obliged to do it every day. "You should talk. Take a turn at it yourself, big mouth."

I swung around and went straight home. Unlike some people I could mention, I don't need anybody's help to amuse myself. I read three books in two days, I showed Zoe how to trace and make a jigsaw puzzle out of a U.S. map, and I shot marbles with the little kids who are her friends. Not for keeps.

You can't play marbles for keeps with little kids.

"Abe came by looking for you," said Mama, looking at me sharply on Friday, when I didn't go out again. "You don't want to see him?"

"I'm busy," I told Mama.

The next time he came by she sent him out into the backyard. Abe stood still, studying me. I was lying on top of the picnic table, reading. I kept on reading.

"How about a game of chess? Just you and me? I'll bring my chess set over."

Abe's set, which he got for a Hanukkah present, is a magnetic one for traveling; he doesn't take it out of the house ordinarily.

"That's not my idea of a fun time," I said without looking up. I once took a book out from the library on how to play chess, but the game is more complicated than checkers. Abe wins most of the time.

Abe sounded a little mad, too, when he answered. "You remind me of what's-his-name, that hero who sulks in his tent? Achilles?"

Because of me, Abe has read all the Greek myths, and now he's reading about the Trojan War, which the ancient Greeks and the Trojans fought for ten years.

"When Achilles did come out of his tent, he got killed. Is that what you have in mind for me? Thanks, but no thanks," I answered.

"You're full of baloney," Abe shouted. He turned,

ran down the slope of our backyard, and jumped from the stone wall to the sidewalk.

"Entertaining you guys every day is a killer of a job, and that's the truth," I yelled out into the empty yard.

Somewhere in the dusk a lonely cat yowled, and an answer came from behind the bushes in our yard. Almost as if they were talking in code. Abe and I used to do that. Talk in code, I mean. I shivered once. The cat yowls were a little creepy in the darkening yard.

When the back door opened and a wide river of light poured out, I moved quickly for the open door. Zoe stood there.

"Suppertime, Zach. Please, pretty please, will you take me to the wooden swings in the big park after supper?" she begged as I went past her. "Pretty please with sugar on it. You know I can't go by myself to the park when it's getting dark."

Well, for somebody who says she needs me, she sure hop-skipped far ahead of me after supper. When I caught up with her at the swings, I gave her a dirty look.

People share the four-seater swings, which have seats facing each other like gliders, and Zoe had jumped on one with Shaky John. Didn't she realize I'd have to pump twice as hard to move the swing? Zoe's legs are too short, and Shaky John couldn't possibly be much use.

Aggravation, that's what Zoe was, aggravation. I said a bad word under my breath.

Shaky John smiled at us. "Ready, k-kids?"

I was still getting set to pump when the swing took off like a rocket, flying up and out. Zoe shrieked in pretended fright and delight.

"T-too high?" asked Shaky John, frowning anxiously across at us.

I shook my head and braced to pump back. Who would have thought that bumbling, shuffling Shaky John had legs of steel? I've never gone so high before, not even with four of us pumping.

As we swung back and forth, I saw him do something else that was puzzling. He kept clamping and unclamping his fingers around the safety bar. Every so often he raised his hands high, then brought them back down to grab the bar. Once he missed. Shaky John's cheeks were red again, but I wasn't sure whether that was from the work of swinging or because he caught me staring.

"It helps to—I—s-strengthen. . . ."

In spite of the unfinished sentences, I understood. He was using the swing as some kind of exercise to help him get control of his muscles. I always thought he came born messed up and couldn't do anything about his condition. But I have to say Shaky John sure made that ride the best ever.

By the time we all walked out of the park, I felt better than I had for two days. Zoe took hold of

Shaky John's hand and chattered like a monkey. Though they walked slowly, I fell behind them on the path. Not because I was worried about anybody seeing me with him. It was more to get a vacation from Zoe's conversation.

Whether it was the swing ride or the walk home that put the idea in Zoe's head, I'm not sure. The next day, she told me this nutty story that Shaky John was some kind of hero. She talked about him doing all kinds of sports and winning everything.

"Zoe, it's okay to imagine things, but when you tell whopping lies, people laugh at you."

"Zachary Athanasius Poulos, you don't know everything. I asked him. He told me so."

I looked at her doubtfully. Shaky John didn't strike me as the kind of person who would tell lies to little kids. It had to be Zoe being Zoe. I wanted to ask Abe what he thought, but then I remembered I was mad at him.

I'll prove it to you, Mr. Smarty," said Zoe indignantly. Her black eyes were snapping with anger, her mouth all pursed up in fury.

"How? You going to have him run a race? Or maybe hit a home run?"

The picture of Shaky John shuffling his way around a field struck even Zoe into silence. She stomped away with her nose up in the air. She didn't speak to me for the rest of the day, not even to say good-night at bedtime.

I don't need Zoe for company, but between her silence and not having Abe around, I was feeling bored brainless. That's why I paid attention the next day when she came flying in from the little park.

"Nyah, nyah, I got it! He did it!" she said excitedly, sticking her tongue out at me.

I can always count on Zoe for a good laugh.

"You got what? Measles or mumps? He-who?"

"Silly Zach. He's waiting in the park. Come see," she answered.

It crossed my mind that maybe she meant Abe, so I let her tug me across the street. But the kids were up by the statue of the Spanish-American War soldier, and Zoe stopped halfway at a bench where Shaky John sat. She plopped herself on the bench and reached into a wagon parked in front of the seat.

"Look, Zach, it's the speedy one with the wings," she said, holding up a shiny gold statuette. "What's his name?"

"Hermes," I answered automatically. That Greek god who acted as messenger for the other gods is easy to recognize because he always has wings on his heels as well as his hat. I frowned as I tried to figure out why Shaky John had this trophy. I mean, it's not your ordinary, everyday decoration for the house.

"Th-tha—tha—it's from B-b-b—" Shaky John gave up trying to talk. Instead, he reached into the wagon and lifted out a large black scrapbook. Open, it stretched across all three of our laps.

" 'Cause you read faster than me, Zach, I'll let you turn the pages," Zoe said generously. "But don't forget to tell me what they say."

What the pages said was that John Talbot was the hero of almost every game he played for his high school and college. There were pictures of him making winning touchdowns, breaking the tape at the end of a race, and doing a swan dive. The picture where he was stretched flat on the football field at his college had the biggest headlines over it.

I read every word of that article about his broken neck and the damage to his spine. The articles that followed were like the stuff you read when somebody has died. From being a champion and a prospect for three events in the Olympics, John Talbot became a person who wasn't expected to ever walk or talk again. I looked at Shaky John and swallowed hard.

"You're better now, aren't you?" I asked thinking of the paragraph that described him as almost totally paralyzed. "When you're all well, will you . . ."

One corner of Shaky John's mouth turned up as he shook his head. "No. No more. This is a-a-bout as g-good as I'll b-be." What I was thinking must have been written across my face. He added, pointing to his head, "I'm okay inside here. The inside is what counts. I'm alive."

What could anybody say after something like that? I'm sorry isn't enough, but I couldn't think of anything else. I don't know when I've had so much on my mind. I never heard the kids who had drifted down by our bench, arguing and yelling. It was Zoe's voice, calling to get their attention, that brought me out of my thoughts.

"See, Shaky John knows all about games and stuff," Zoe announced to them. She waved smugly at the scrapbook and the trophy.

"I bet he never heard of a game where you climb trees to knock on old ladies' windows and scare them," said Abe, eyeing Wylie Bowen. "Old Mrs. Murphy never did anything to you."

"You afraid of a little climbing? You're so full of ideas, what's better?" Wylie sneered.

That was a dirty crack. Abe is not chicken, but he's not exactly what you'd call athletic.

A slow smile started spreading across my face. It's not often that you get an idea that's perfect in every way. Not only did I know something better than Wylie Bowen's plan, it was something that was going to help me decide about what to be when I'm grown up.

"Everybody, listen. We start now and we've got all summer to work on it and train for it," I annouced. "You know how the Olympic Games got canceled on account of the war in Europe? Well, we are going to put on our own junior Olympics. "Sha . . . John Talbot"—at this point I waved at Shaky John—"will be coach and referee for us. Look through his scrapbook and see how he knows about training, practice, and winning."

For a minute I wondered. Should I have asked him first? But when I looked at him, it was all right. John had a wide grin, and his head was bobbing up and down in agreement.

With cries of "Yeah," and "Wow," kids were leafing through the scrapbook as Wylie, standing by himself, muttered under his breath. Chuckling, I said, "Remember that famous saying, Wylie: You can't judge a book by its cover."

Although I had stopped Wylie Bowen dead, Abe didn't look thrilled. That's when I got my second inspiration. Sometimes I astonish even myself. I made my next announcement. "Attention, everybody. We are going to make our Olympics brawn *and* brain contests. We'll have chess and checkers tournaments, too."

"Zach, what's brawn? I don't understand," said Zoe.

"Another word for muscles, Zoe. Some people have those in their heads as well as their arms and legs," explained Abe, laughing.

2
Testing: One, Two, Three

Resting on the bottom in the green gloom, I had shut my eyes. From somewhere above, the words "Let's . . . sub . . . marine . . ." sank slowly to my ears. Curiosity made me open my eyes to see who was coming down to join me, but I saw only pink white legs swim past my nose. Kicking hard with both legs, I raised my left arm and got a sharp pain on the back of my hand. I shot up and out of the water.

Just as I thought. I'd scraped against the cement column in the center of the wading pool. Standing up in the water that reached to my waist, I sucked my sore knuckles. The wading pool below Elk Street has more water in it than most, but only somebody Zoe's size can do anything in such a dinky pool and shallow water.

"Watch, Zack. I'm going underwater," Zoe called. Pinching her nose shut, she ducked her head into the water and out faster than the human eye can blink. "Did you see me swim underwater?" she yelled, jumping up and down.

"You'll never get in our Olympics that way," I said. "C'mon, I'll help you to submarine."

The happy, triumphant smile on Zoe's face disappeared, and for a second I felt lower than a snake's belly. Still, she's the one who insists on sticking with me and my friends, so she's got to learn, I told myself.

"It's good practice. Remember, you have to do dead man's float at the Red Cross lessons," I reminded her, and braced myself, my legs apart for her to dive through.

A look of pure fright crossed Zoe's face. I don't remember ever being that scared to put my head underwater. Patty, who takes Zoe with her to the free lessons at the Olympic-size pool in Lincoln Park, says everybody in the Minnows has trouble with that part.

I didn't want to stand around all day coaxing her, so I said, "Look, Zoe, what's that floating there by my feet?"

Zoe bent her head a tiny bit, trying to see what I was pointing at.

"No, no, you have to get down closer to the water to see it."

Zoe bent from the waist, putting her face within an inch of the water. Still frowning, she peered hard. "I don't see . . . *glub-ub*."

With a hand on each shoulder, I had given her a hard shove under the water. Then I pushed her bottom through my legs. I turned around in time to see a panting, sputtering Zoe shoot out of the water.

"You almost drownded me," she yelled, and hammered on my chest with both fists.

"But you didn't drown. And you finally went underwater that time like a real swimmer, so what are you complaining about?"

Zoe was in no mood to be reasonable. She splashed her face with water to clear the salty tears and spit great mouthfuls of water at me like an angry whale. The idea of peanut-sized Zoe as a whale made me burst out laughing, which didn't help matters. Zoe turned her back on me and slogged out of the water without another word. Only God and Zoe knew what she'd tell Mama, but I'd worry about that when I got home.

My more important worry was how to train enough to stay ahead of everybody for the swimming competition. If only I could talk Mama into letting me skip work. . . . It was worth a try, so I gave it my best at suppertime.

"Whoa, Zachary. Talking ninety-nine times faster than usual does not bring you an answer any sooner," said Papa, rubbing his head and messing the hair that covers his bald spot. After loading ships all day at the Port of Albany, Papa always washes up and combs his hair before coming to work the night shift at our store.

"Somebody has to take orders out front during the noon rush hour. Do you want your papa to be the one? To give up the work that helps the war effort and your cousins in Greece?" Mama said. "Besides, I don't like you going in such deep water as the big pool."

Our store has only six stools at the counter and one table, but it gets busier than a bus station at noon. When she put it that way, what could I say? I had to remind her at least that a) I'm an intermediate swimmer, so worrying about deep water was a waste of time and b) everybody else I know gets to go practically every morning for lessons and some kids spend the whole day at the pool.

"Intermediate is nothing," Mama said practically snorting. "Remember the story of Leander and Hero? Leander was expert swimming every night across the miles of the Hellespont to visit Hero but still one night Leander drowned."

Sometimes I wish the old Greeks hadn't written so many stories or at least that my folks hadn't read every single one of them.

Papa exchanged a look with Mama, who bit her lip and asked, "Still, you can go afterwards, can't you?"

I shrugged. "By the time I walk over there, it's almost time for the whistle to get out. And you know unless we're with a grown-up, we can't stay or go back in the pool after four-thirty."

With so many dumb rules in the parks and play-grounds, it's a wonder you ever see any kids in them. Just on account of that pool rule, every kid under sixteen is always home way before supper.

Mama said, "Too much. *Zaharia*, it's too much for me alone to take orders, cook, wash dishes, and load the soda cooler. There is no question of choice in this."

Mama had pulled her lips into a single tight line, a sign that she was losing her temper. Or maybe she felt guilty about making her child work when others weren't?

"How is it if we let you quit work by one, one-thirty?" offered Papa. "And each time you go, you get twenty cents to ride over on the trolley car? Then you have more time in the pool."

Boy! I never meant to get money out of them, too. Papa's offer made me feel like a blackmailer but not guilty enough to refuse the money. Instead, I promised myself silently to split fifty-fifty with Zoe if I saved any of the money for snacks. Mumbling thanks, I left the supper table before the blanket of guilt smothered me.

Whether I walk or ride, I always put my bathing suit on at home under my clothes. That way I don't waste time at the pool changing. I just drop my clothes in the wire basket, get my metal locker tag, and head straight into the water. My suit is an old-fashioned, itchy wool one. Mama sewed a new suit, two pieces, for Zoe. I don't want a homemade suit, but I sure would like to have a suit for our Olympics that's more up to date.

Our crowd usually settles on the sand beach that's just in front of where the grass starts. Farther up on the grassy hill the teenagers sit. Sometimes you find a couple behind one of the bushes there, making googly eyes at one another, holding hands and even kissing.

I know I'll never be that dumb.

Today, after running through the showers, I checked around for Patty and Zoe. Patty's dark cherry-colored hair makes her easy to pick out. I spotted them surrounded by little kids about Zoe's age. All the little kids were tipping over and tumbling on the sand like drunken sailors.

Patty, who was steadying an upside-down kid's legs, explained, "They're practicing somersaults, cartwheels, and standing on their heads for the Olympics. Zoe said they could all sign up."

I grunted. "And who gave her the right to make decisions?"

Zoe was stuck halfway through a somersault. Her upside-down face between her legs was tomato red as she strained to heave herself over the rest of the way.

"Upsy daisy," I said and flipped her over.

Zoe came right-side up, looking as cross as a crab. She said, "I can do it my ownself. Don't touch me. I don't want you to talk to me, either."

Turning her back on me, she linked her arm with a dark-haired girl about her age. "Gina, I know lots of stories and good things to do. *You* can be my friend."

Frankly, I thought Gina, who tried to tug her arm free, seemed more scared than pleased by the honor Zoe had given her.

"Listen, this is a joke, Gina," Zoe announced. "What do ghosts eat for supper? Make a guess."

One second later, Zoe said, "Give up? Ghosts eat spook-getti for supper."

Gina giggled. Zoe shot a quick look at me to see if I was impressed. Then Zoe herself started giggling, which set Gina off again. Finally, the two headed for the water arm-in-arm. I've noticed that sharing a laugh often cements two people together.

"Zoe has to be told she can't pick who'll be in the Olympics," I said to Patty.

"Zach, why can't you let her be in charge of some of the little kids?" Patty asked.

"Because we got a committee, that's why. And we all agreed that the committee decides. If *I* say Zoe can run the little kids, everybody will accuse me of bossing the whole show." I was annoyed. Usually I don't have to spell things out with Patty.

"But you know Zoe gets a lot of ideas. She's like

you," Patty commented. "So, it's natural for her to copy the way you behave, to take charge."

I exploded. "D'you realize what you just said? Here I am, going out of my way to let everybody have a part, and you attack me again for being too bossy."

"Well, Mr. Grouchy, didn't you this minute say Zoe *can't* be in charge of the six-year-olds?" Patty snapped back at me.

I was still steaming over the injustice of it as I went into the water, looking for Abe Zalkin. Lincoln is a gigantic circular pool. We go just past the ropes into water that's chin-high on both of us. Then we swim all the way around the pool to build speed and endurance. I can tell I'm improving. I stopped only four times to catch my breath.

When Abe caught up with me, he was gasping. "Time for a break. I gotta buy some energy or something," he said.

"Let's lie in the sun till we decide what to get," I suggested.

On the beach, I forgot to shake out the towel before I laid down. That was my first, but not my last big mistake of the day. Sand stuck to me all over, even creeping into my bathing suit. I didn't dare scratch, though. A person watching might get the idea that I had bugs or lice.

"Who is Zoe talking to?" Abe asked.

I squinted against the sun to see. Zoe was between

Patty and a blanket full of strange girls. "Nobody I recognize."

I almost laughed out loud. Louie the Lip had come up silently behind Patty with a bathing cap full of water. Raising his arms up high, he got ready to dump it. A girl on the blanket screamed a warning, and Patty rolled away in the nick of time. From her shriek, you would have thought Patty had been drenched, not just splashed. Jumping up, the girls tugged the blanket to a different spot and offered Patty sympathy and dry towels. All the while they kept eyeing Louie and giggling.

Abe gave a low whistle. "Did you see how much hair Louie's got under his arms?"

I had noticed. "It's not so much. Mostly, you see it because his hair is so black."

Since I have light, straw-colored hair, new hairs on me don't show up so much as some people's. My hair and golden brown eyes surprise people who think all Greeks are dark like Zoe. I wanted to ask Abe if he's seen any changes in his own body. But that's real private stuff, too embarrassing to talk about. Instead I stood up and told him I'd be right back.

The need to scratch was driving me crazy. Even the inside of my throat itched! I ran to the top of the teenagers' favorite grassy hill. Behind some bushes I hopped up and down, shaking off the sand and scratching hard all over. Then I loosened the drawstring on my bathing suit and brushed off the inside of me. I took the long way coming back down, but I didn't see anything interesting.

As I rejoined Abe, the strangest thing happened. I blinked and looked again at the blanket where the girls sat with their backs to me. For one split second, I had thought the girl who was undoing her braids was naked! Really naked. In a *public* pool.

Then I realized she had an all-over honey tan and her bathing suit was the same color as her skin. Even more amazing, the hair that she was loosening to dry was a honey color, too. I never saw anything like it.

Abe's elbow in my ribs took me by surprise. "Zach, can't you hear? I said, are you coming or not?"

As we left, I looked back. Wylie Bowen was moving toward the group. If those girls wanted to giggle at something, they should look at Wylie's pear shape, I thought.

"We use my three cents for penny candy and maybe get a chocolate bar with your nickel?" Abe asked as we wound our way through the locker room and out of the bathhouse to the refreshment stand.

"Hey, boy, *pos pas ke pou pas?*"

Abe, who recognizes Greek now when he hears it, asked me, "Is that peanut man who's talking to you Mr. Brown?" Then Abe snickered.

Abe thinks it's funny that a Greek is named Mr. Brown, but I don't. Years ago, when immigration

41

officers on Ellis Island didn't understand what people from the Old Country were saying, they sometimes took the easy way out in writing down the people's names. You can guess what color Mr. Brown was wearing on the day he came through. Even my family's name got shortened from Keramopoulos to Poulos.

"Uh-uh," I said after a quick look. "Mr. Brown only sells in Washington Park. That's George, the Cypriote."

Politely—Mama would skin me alive if I wasn't—I stopped by the peanut cart to answer him. "I'm fine, thank you, *Kyrie Georgio*. And we're on the way to buy something because we're hungry."

"Oh, we take care of hungry boys right here." George smiled as he filled the big ten-cent size bag with roasted peanuts in the shell.

Abe tried to tug me away, hissing that I promised to get candy, not peanuts. Ignoring him, I said, "Thank you," twice, once in English and once in Greek.

"That little detour was A-okay," Abe admitted on our way back over the hot sand. Besides the peanuts, we carried bags of penny candy and a Hershey bar. Abe couldn't get over what he called our good luck. George had refused to take any money from us for the peanuts.

I snorted. "It wasn't luck—I planned that stop. I knew he would do that. I've told you and told you:

Greeks are hospitable people. They're always treating other Greeks. Speaking of which . . ."

I meant to ask him if we should offer something to the girls sitting near our stuff, but I got sidetracked. Wylie Bowen still stood by their blanket, his hands on his hips, posing, kind of. He must have thought the pose showed off his muscles, which I'm here to tell you don't exist. Actually, the girls were watching Zoe and Gina.

"Pay 'tention, everybody," Zoe commanded as she and Gina faced us and the group on the blanket. "This is Zachary Athanasius Poulos when he went up behind the bushes."

She and Gina danced around as if they had ants in their pants. Scratching their stomachs and chests with both hands, they looked like crazy monkeys. Their audience roared with laughter.

That wasn't the worst of it. Wylie Bowen decided to get in the act. He copied Zoe and Gina, dancing around, scratching exactly like them. If the two girls had looked like crazy monkeys, he reminded me of an oversized baboon.

I couldn't let him get away with it. There was only one course of action open to me. I tensed my muscles to go after Wylie. Zoe, I would deal with later on the way home. Through the fog in my ears, I heard one of the girls say, "What a dummy, imitating an imitation," and she turned her back on him.

43

The honey-colored girl—I still couldn't see her face—was rubbing suntan oil on her stretched-out legs, and I realized that in fact, *all the girls were ignoring Wylie.*

I thanked my stars, because suddenly I saw an even better way to deal with him. Offering Patty the peanuts, I acted as if Wylie Bowen didn't exist. "Too, too childish," I said, smiling and nodding at Zoe and Gina to indicate that I was talking about them.

When I got to Zoe, I hesitated. The last thing I wanted was to reward her for spying on me. Still, I had promised myself to share fifty-fifty with her. I hate people who break promises, so I took out one peanut and handed it to her. Zoe didn't look at me as she took it.

"Zach, you haven't had any yourself," said Patty.

"I'm going back in the water, so I don't want to eat anything now," I lied. What I really wanted was to put some distance between those girls and myself. I don't trust girls. Who knows who or what they might find funny next.

Just then the lifeguards blew their whistles to clear the pool of kids. The girls collected their stuff and left so fast I never did get around the blanket to see the honey-colored girl's face.

"By the way," said Abe, I liked the way you treated Wylie. Slicker than oil."

"I don't want to walk home with him. Let's wait a bit."

We sat on the curb of the pool with the afternoon sun toasting our backs. Seeing John Talbot shuffling along the walk toward us reminded me.

"Abe, what events—besides the chess, I mean—are you going to try for?" I asked.

We already decided that Abe, who has a loud voice like Donald Duck, should be an announcer for the games. But he never had said what else he wanted to do.

"Um . . . maybe one of the uh, races?"

I didn't know what to say. He probably couldn't beat me swimming, and Patty Zelda Aylward is the speediest runner I ever met. No way Abe could beat her, either. But that's not the kind of thing you want to tell a best friend.

John and a lifeguard both reached us at the same time. It was the head lifeguard, and he waved his whistle at us in a shooing motion. "You're under sixteen, kids, so beat it home."

"We are, but he isn't," I said, pointing to John.

"You're telling me you're with him?" asked the lifeguard in a voice that said he didn't believe me. "Next, you'll tell me he's your uncle."

I opened my eyes wide and said as sincerely as I could, "Oh, that would be a lie. I wouldn't do that." I sneaked a look at John's face to see how far I could go. "But he *is* our coach, and we're in training."

"So tell me the names of these guys who're on your team," he said, challenging John directly.

I held my breath. Would John be willing to act as if we were with him? Did he even know all our names?

John said, "The one with the mop of c-curly hair is Abe, the light-haired one is Zach, and the little b-brunette one—be-believe it or not—is Zach's sister. They don't look at all alike, do they?"

Whew. Saved. We could stay another whole hour, until five-thirty at least. John must listen a lot while he sits on the park bench.

"Oh, and don't forget Patty Aylward—the girl over there—is with us, too," I added.

Once the guard had left, Abe and I slapped each other on the back. "Yah-hoo! We did it," I exclaimed. Turning, I said to John, "You're a true-blue friend." I meant what I said, too, though normally, I wouldn't think of counting a grown-up as a friend.

"Only now you have a lot more to do," said John. "You're in t-training, remember? So b-back into the water, you g-go. Smooth out your strokes."

"You're kidding," I said, looking up at John. As usual, he was smiling, but it was a steely kind of smile, I thought. "You're *not* kidding," I exclaimed after a second look at his face.

"You're in t-training . . . you said it, not me," John reminded me.

He knew, or should have known, that I had only

said the bit about training so we could stay longer at the pool. I scowled.

"Or would you rather b-be called a liar?"

"I'm all swum out," I snapped, and that was no lie. But most of all, I don't like being told like some little kid that I haven't done enough homework.

"In swim meets, no one asks if you're t-tired or if you want to wait and race another day," John pointed out. "If you'd rather not c-compete, you can always sit on the side and time the races."

When it was *my* idea to have an Olympics contest, he thought I would sit on the sidelines? I opened my mouth to tell John he was nuts.

Wylie Bowen, who came by just then, warned, "Zach, if I can't pass for older, you sure can't. That head lifeguard will be checking on you next. You might as well get up now."

"The guard already did, Wylie," I answered without looking at John Talbot. "But we, um, have a grown-up who, uh, sponsored us."

Tweet . . . tweet . . . tweet. When the head lifeguard finally took the whistle out of his mouth, he yelled, "You, in the yellow trunks, I told you once already—out. If I have to come after you, I'll make you stay out of the pool a whole week."

Wylie gave us a dirty look as if—somehow—we were to blame. Dragging his towel on the ground, he headed slowly for the bathhouse. I sighed. If it weren't for John, we'd be walking out right along-side Wylie. Without a word, I turned away and went into the water.

I simmered at a slow boil all the way around the pool. I didn't even realize until I reached my start-ing point that I had stopped just twice this time around. Nobody else noticed.

Abe was swimming doggedly back and forth on the shallow side of the ropes between two posts. Zoe, legs stretched out behind her, was doing her duck-the-head-in-and-out act. John kept a hand under her stomach to assure her she wouldn't sink. Actually, she held her full face in the water for more than a second now, I noticed.

At-choo. Zoe's head came out of the water just in time to blow a great granddaddy of a sneeze.

I said out loud to no one in particular, "D'you know how tough it is to swim when you're so tired?"

John looked over at me and said quietly, "I—I know how hard it is to t-try . . . when you're t-tired."

I didn't need Abe's startled look or Zoe's re-proachful black eyes to tell me. This, my second mistake of the day, was a real whopper. I felt small. Bug-size small. Microscope-size small. What a stu-pid thing for me to say.

I tried to explain. "I mean . . . I like learning, but once you know the stroke, doing it over and over is boring and wears you out. I, um, guess I'd rather be racing."

John's face broke open in a big grin. "Zach, my c-coach used to remind us every day: An Indian has to learn to be an Indian before he can be a chief."

"Okay, this Indian brave has put himself chest deep in learning," I joked. "So you can relax and take a swim yourself."

I felt the sweat spring out on my forehead. Lordy, but my tongue was determined to embarrass me into a grave today. I never noticed if John does any swimming when he's at the pool. Or if he can.

Lucky for me he had other things on his mind. He turned to Abe and said, "Don't thrash so. Work on your k-k . . . move your legs in rhythm. Hold onto the rope and do only that."

"John has more patience than any grown-up I've ever met," said Patty from behind me. "Don't you think?"

I didn't answer. I was watching John plunge into the water and head for the diving raft in the middle of the pool. He covered more distance in three strokes than anybody I've ever seen. In the water you couldn't even tell that his muscles don't always obey him. It must have taken more than patience, more like buckets of guts for him to get so he could do that.

Zoe called out, "Patty, c'n you help me? I wanna try again. . . ."

Patty, who was frog-kicking away from our group in a backstroke, never heard her. Left behind in the shallow water, Zoe looked a little like an orphan.

"Somebody," she called again, "somebody help me. I got nobody."

Of all the silly things to say when I was standing right there. I took a breath, a deep one, and said, "Zoe, I'll do tugboat with you. Put your face in, with your arms straight out, and I'll tow you."

Zoe looked doubtful, but at last she gingerly put her face down in the water, and I started towing her. In a minute she lifted her head and opened her eyes. When she saw how far we'd traveled, she got excited and started kicking her legs.

Finally, I gave her advance notice. "Zoe, I'm going to let go of your fingertips for just a second to scratch my nose. You won't sink, I promise."

Zoe kept on kicking automatically, and before I finished scratching she had swum at least three yards away on her own power. Startled, she put her feet down and touched bottom. Then she yelled at the top of her lungs, "Hey, everybody, hey! I'm a Tadpole now, not a Minnow."

John, Abe, and Patty had come back in time to hear her, and we all laughed at the same time. Mama says I'm too quick . . . too quick to jump into doing things, into making up my mind, into everything. She may be right. Because just now I was with the majority, and it felt good.

"Zach, you need to . . . when you lift your head

out to b-breathe, turn your head only. Hold your b-body straight. Try it out to the raft and back. I'll watch and keep reminding you," said John.

I didn't know what to say. I mean, I don't go to the raft. Sometimes I end up swimming in water a little over my head when I go around the pool, but I don't go out to the raft. It's more like kids in high school who do that. I'm not scared. I honestly and truly think a guy ought to be at least thirteen to go out to the raft. My birthday isn't for another couple of weeks.

John had that steely smile on his face again as he added, "I'll swim right b-beside you all the way."

I couldn't think of a way to explain to John. We continued to stand in what seemed like a pool of silence.

Abe broke it up by saying in a too loud voice, "Maybe you oughtta save that trip for another day. Little by little is my motto."

John didn't take his eyes off my face as he answered, "A b-better motto is: Never p-put off till tomorrow what can be done today."

I cleared my throat to make my voice work.

John's voice dropped lower as if to share a secret. "Somebody has to go first. If you don't, who else . . . ?"

He didn't say anything more. But he knew and I knew that Abe would never try it before I did. If I held back, so would Abe, and maybe even Patty, too. Out by the raft, I could see a lifeguard in a rowboat, keeping an eye on the divers and swimmers. It's really deep out there.

"Going out to the raft will make me late for supper," I pointed out.

"Wait till I tell Mama. Just like Zachary, I can go in water over my head now," Zoe boasted to Patty.

I saw no way out. Taking a deep breath, I kicked off from the pole. I reached out, with my arms up, out, and down into the water for what seemed like forever. Each time I turned my head to breathe, I could see John nearby as he'd promised.

"Ouch!" Sooner than I expected the raft was in front of me. I'd whacked my hand against it. John, who was already there, wasn't even breathing heavily. We both hung onto the side for a bit. After I caught my breath, I signaled John that I was ready to swim back.

Funny how the distance looked really short now. I was actually enjoying myself on the return trip. That made it all the worse when the horror struck.

My brain froze and unfroze all in the same instant. My rhythm broke down, and I treaded water frantically, trying to decide where to put my hands. Nobody else had seen anything. Nobody else could help. Only I could rescue myself. Speed was crucial.

Grimly I hurled myself forward again. I heard John's voice far off, but I knew it would be fatal to slow or stop to listen. Minutes, days, years later my feet touched bottom. Instantly I wrapped both arms tightly around my waist, my hands clutching my suit.

From behind the ropes, Abe called out, "Jeez, Zach, you moved faster than a V-2 rocket bomb. You even beat John."

John's eyes were wide with surprise and worry when he asked, "You okay, Zach?" Eyeing my arms hugging my body, he added, "D-did you get a cramp?"

I hung somewhere between wanting to laugh and wanting to cry. Moving only my head, I beckoned John to come closer. I whispered my answer.

"What did you say?" John leaned closer to hear.

My voice was unsteady from the shock of what had nearly happened. I whispered again. "The drawstring . . . broke. My suit almost . . ."

John never made a sound, but his shoulders shook like a bowl of jelly. Then he leaned over again and whispered back, "Zach, it actually happened once to me. But I didn't *know* I'd lost my b-bathing suit. I climbed up on the raft b-bare as the day I was b-born."

"Wh-what did you do?" I asked.

John answered shaking his head, "What c-could I do? I yelled to a friend on the beach to bring me a towel and dove back in. Then I treaded water until I got it to wrap around me."

In my mind's eye I saw him on the raft, tall and proud and . . . naked. I shuddered and almost let go of my suit. "Guts, John. You've got buckets of guts."

Now John did roar out loud with laughter, and I joined in. Patty, Zoe, and Abe stood looking at us in that stiff way of people who've been left out of a joke. I didn't intend to explain it to them, either.

Finally we stopped laughing. When John spoke, he surprised me so much that again I almost let go of my suit.

"Zach, my mother never throws anything out. I think we have some racer's t-trunks in small sizes that you can have. I'll stop at your store with them tonight."

Part of my surprise was his mentioning his mother. I never thought about John having a family. I guess I never thought past what I saw: a guy on a park bench who walks and talks funny. Come to think of it, there was another surprise. The longer I knew and listened to John, the less I heard his stutter.

But what a break. To own a real racer's suit, one that's been worn by a winner. Who knows what kind of luck that suit might bring me? And now that I'd been out to the raft, I could learn to do real dives. Hanging onto the top of my no-waist suit, I called thanks over my shoulder to John and headed for the locker room.

I changed behind the door of one of the bathroom

stalls where no one could see me and rolled my old wool suit up in the towel. Mama might want to use it for rags or patching something. Closing the stall door behind me, I rapped on the wood three times for luck.

On the way home Patty got annoyed with me. "Zach, you're a slowpoke today. Why are you being so careful and taking so long to cross at each corner?"

Why? Why, because if I got hit, I'd have to go to the hospital. In the hospital they undress you for the doctors to examine. And, since I had worn my suit over to Lincoln, I didn't have any underwear on. But I couldn't tell Patty that.

"Why?" I answered finally. "Because I just can't afford to get run over."

3
A Racing Tongue

Rotten is how I feel. Lousy. I wonder how many words there are in the dictionary for feeling bad. A zillion wouldn't be enough to cover my condition.

For one thing, my throat feels as if I'd swallowed too much chlorine water, and I haven't even been swimming for three days. For another thing, I am hot. Even my eyeballs are sweating. And the inside of my head is having its own private Fourth of July celebration. Every time I turn or move, firecrackers explode.

Maybe I'd stayed up too late last night reading *The Princess of Mars*. Ordinarily, I don't read books with *Princess* in the title, but this has a lot of good stuff about life on Mars. It's by the guy who wrote the Tarzan books. Wouldn't it be something if people could really go out traveling in space? I wonder if Abe knows if it could happen. He follows the war news every day, so he's kind of an expert on planes and rockets.

A bang . . . inside my head? Outside? The noise

sounded a lot like a refrigerator door opening and closing. Not just once, but over and over. I finally figured out that the slamming sound was coming through my ears. Nobody was in the store but me and Zoe. Mama had gone to pay bills. Slowly I got up from the table, and slowly I put my head around the kitchen partition to investigate.

Sure enough, Zoe stood in front of the refrigerator, holding the door open a crack. Her nose was stuck in the crack. Suddenly, she pulled back and slammed the door shut. Then just as quickly she yanked it open again.

"Zoe, are you trying to break the refrigerator?"

Zoe jumped and slammed the door shut again. She spun around and said, "You scared me. You almost made me nearly shut my fingers in the door. Stop yelling."

"What are you doing?" I added, "Almost doesn't count."

"Oh, so you want me to really cut off my fingers?"

"Zoe, that's *not* the question. The question is: What are you doing to the refrigerator?" Now I was truly yelling. Sometimes I think I'm the only sane one in my family.

"I'm doing a 'speriment, so leave me alone," she yelled back.

"You're not allowed to. At least not experiments that wreck the refrigerator. If you stand with the door open—"

"You aren't the only one who can find answers to everything," she shouted. "I can think for my own self. I'm going into second grade, you know."

"The whole world knows it now, Zoe," Mama observed. Frowning, she closed the screen door behind her and said, "This is a place of business, not a playground for screaming and fighting children. Zachary, what have you been doing?"

Talk about jumping to conclusions! How come I was the one who had to answer?

"I've been doing exactly what I was told to do," I snapped, giving Zoe a dirty look. "Minding the store, which today means keeping Zoe from knocking the place down."

"Liar! I wasn't knocking anything. I was learning." She glanced sideways at Mama. I have to hand it to Zoe. She knows Mama loves learning more than anything. "I only tried to see if the light stays on after you close the door."

"It doesn't," Mama said, half-smiling for one moment. With a sigh she took her apron off the hook, tied it around her waist, and added, "Zoe, clear the table for supper. Zach, go pick parsley and lettuce for salad from the garden. Stay out there a while and, uh, tie up the cucumber vines, too."

I can take a hint. After I dumped the salad on the countertop, I went back out to the yard. Lying on top of the picnic table, I cooled off a little. By the time I came back in, Papa was at the table, ready for supper.

"Climbing up the path to being a man, the way is foggy with much stumbling and false trails. And *Zaharia* has first to separate himself from us," said Papa.

Me. They were talking about me. Where did Papa think I should go to separate myself? He wasn't making a whole lot of sense.

Mama replied, "Yes, yes, but tonight it's more like he's sickening with something. Why, he didn't even talk back when I sent him to the garden."

She hates to think Zoe and I aren't best buddies. Whenever Mama catches us quarreling, she's positive that it's because one of us is sick.

Brushing past Mama to my seat on the end, I said, "The only disease I've got is called lack of money. It's Zoe who suffers from a serious illness. She's just a baby, but thinks she's a queen bee. Excuse my mistake. I should say a spoiled-rotten queen."

Besides salad, supper was a big bowl of noodles with butter, oil, and Greek feta cheese crumbled all over it. I pushed the noodles around on my plate and wondered if I could get any down. My throat felt like it had a big glob of something foreign in it.

Zoe's indignant, "I am not," was muffled as she

slurped noodles. "I'm growing every day. You watch, I won't be the baby anymore. Then we'll see who's boss of who."

"Zoe, get it through your head once and for all: You got born after me, way after me. That'll never change. You'll always be the baby of our family."

That reminded me. I put two fingers up above my upper lip and felt around carefully. This morning when I looked in the mirror, I could have sworn I saw a couple of hairs, but I couldn't find them now. It's a worrisome thing. If my body doesn't hurry up, the other guys will all have their grown-up voices before mine even starts to change.

"Who did you pick on before you had me?" Zoe asked, her voice sulky because she knew I was right.

"Not nice, *Zaharia*," said Mama and advanced on me. She pulled my head toward her and put her lips to my forehead. Not to kiss me. It's her way of checking to see if we have a temperature. Mama claims it's more reliable than any thermometer.

Now she drew back as if she'd touched a toad. "*Zaharia*, how long have you been running a fever?"

For a smart lady, Mama sometimes asks dumb questions. How should I know?

She didn't wait for an answer. "Home. Pajamas and bed. As soon as I clean up here, I'll be there to give you aspirin and juice."

I made a face. Drinking orange juice sounded

about as good to me as swallowing a pot of poison would.

"Wait," said Papa to Mama.

"Wait?" For what 'wait'?"

Mama looked as surprised as I felt. Papa almost never steps in after Mama's given me an order.

Outside our store, the sign says POP'S PLACE, but inside the store everything is fifty-fifty. Both Papa and Mama cook, both sweep and clean, both decide how to divide up the money for bills and stuff. Still, things to do strictly with me and Zoe—like sewing clothes and taking temperatures—is Mama's business only.

"Since Easter, how many times is it that Zach has been sick?" Papa asked.

Mama frowned. "Since Easter . . . three. And this makes four."

The screen door slammed as a customer came in. Papa looked up and said to Bud Fenner, the carpenter who's a regular customer, "Be with you in a minute, Buddy. We got a problem here to solve."

"You want to hammer something out?" Buddy asked, chuckling and patting his tool apron with the hammer in the corner pocket.

Bud's jokes aren't great. He's terrific about doing things with his hands, though. He found a junky old wagon and fixed it like new for me. Now I make money sometimes delivering an order for the meat market. And when Zoe's *Evzona* doll, the Greek soldier, lost its arms, Buddy said a soldier shouldn't have to fight without arms. He carved new ones for the doll.

"They're counting up how many times I've been sick," I explained to Bud. "If they go back to January, you'll be waiting a while."

"If we count from January, we'll need two hands," said Mama, "I told you I don't like you going all the way to the big pool. Besides the water being so deep, you must have got a chill coming home."

Buddy, who always sits on the last stool at the counter, swiveled to look at me. Then he spoke to Papa in a sharp voice, "Zach running a temperature? And you say he's been swimming?"

The silence in the store was so deep and so loud, it practically hurt my ears. Why did the three of them look so alarmed?

"Well, I guess I better get going home to bed," I said breaking the silence.

"No," said Mama, her arm snaking out to stop me and keep me at the table. If I didn't already have a headache, Mama's seesawing back and forth in her orders was enough to give me one.

"Stay until Papa comes back," she said, then turned to Papa. "*Thanassi*, go next door to Joe's newsroom. Phone to the doctor. Tell him . . . about the swimming. Ask how quickly he can come." Mama was chewing hard on her lower lip all the

62

while she spoke. "Zoe, don't sit so close to Zach. Come around to this side of the table."

Wow. I wondered if I had the Black Death or something. I wished I could see myself in the mirror. But, mostly, I wished I didn't feel so crummy.

"We've had nothing in this part of the country for at least two summers, and I haven't seen any stories in the newspaper or warnings about a new outbreak, so don't jump the gun," said Buddy to Mama after Papa hurried out.

"Who's got a gun?" asked Mama, looking confused. Mama's English is sort of okay except when she gets excited. And, of course, she doesn't know anything about races or a starter's gun.

"I mean, let the doctor decide what Zach has," Buddy answered. He looked at me and asked cautiously, "You, uh, breathing all right? Your legs, um, feel okay?"

"Of course. My throat hurts, that's all," I answered crossly. Why should my sore throat make him so nervous?

"And the temperature. He has the temperature. That's how it started for President Roosevelt, yes?" asked Mama.

I've heard of delirium, which is a form of going crazy, but I never expected to experience it myself. What did President Franklin Delano Roosevelt have to do with my sore throat?

Papa came back in looking more worried than

when he left. "The doctor is out making visits to patients. I told the nurse and she promises to tell the doctor as soon as she finds him."

"But if it's late when she finds him, after Joe has closed the newsroom? How will the doctor talk to us? You must go sit at the doctor's door," said Mama.

Papa patted Mama on the shoulder. "Not to worry, Joe says. He'll stay and do his bills until the doctor phones back. You get Zach into bed. No matter what the doctor says, *Zaharia* will need rest in bed."

"The thing to remember about Roosevelt," said Buddy, "is even though—or after he got the braces—he got to be President of the United States."

I never thought about being that when I grow up. Was he saying being sick helped Roosevelt to become president? I didn't get it, but for once in my life I didn't care if my curiosity never got satisfied. My only wish now was to get to bed, so I said goodnight and moved out fast.

Once I woke up to hear the doctor's voice saying that my walking to the bathroom proved something. But I didn't hear what it proved. Another time in that crazy mixed-up night, I woke to see Mama on her knees in front of the icon in the kitchen. She kept crossing herself, murmuring, and touching her forehead to the floor like those people in fairy tales who beg favors from the king. I'm not sure, but I think I heard her crying, too.

Mama lights that candle in front of our holy picture every night, not just Saturdays and Saints' days, because Zoe and I are home alone until they close the store at midnight. When Zoe starts worrying about robbers, I prove to her by that light that there are none hiding in the kitchen.

I slept a lot. A whole week, days and nights, in fact.

"You missed the parade on the Fourth of July, Zach," said Zoe from the doorway to my room. All parades pass down Central Avenue to the capitol. The Fourth draws the biggest crowds and is one of our busiest days in the store.

"Papa said I was a big help to Mama. I gave out the soda straws and even rang up on the cash register. Is that okay with you?"

My lips and tongue were drier than a desert. I shook my head. At least it no longer hurt when I moved. "Zoe, you don't need my permission . . . to work."

"I don't want you mad at me," she said anxiously. "Mama fixed you a basket, and I carried it all the way upstairs. There's rice pudding and grapes. Do you want me to unplug some of the grapes for you? Mama says if you need something, I should run and tell her."

It was spooky. A Zoe anxious and willing to do

whatever I asked? It was like living with someone trying out for angelhood. But I didn't understand then how scared everybody had been.

When I finally got out of bed and out of the house, Abe said to me, "How come you yourself didn't worry about polio? You know, it's the catchiest disease ever. That's why they close down swimming pools as soon as someone gets it. Anyway, you should have caught on when they talked about President Roosevelt."

"Listen, with a temperature as high as mine and a throat as sore as what I had, my brain wasn't exactly in tip-top shape, either. Besides, how was I to know that Roosevelt is paralyzed from polio? The newspapers never ever show pictures of him standing with those iron braces."

"Well, seems as if I've known all my life about him being paralyzed. Good thing we don't have any polio going around right now," Abe said, finally giving up the argument. "Did the doctor say you absolutely have to have your tonsils out? And when?"

"My mother says she never wants to live through a night like that again. I don't get any choice. They're gonna yank them this coming Monday."

I've asked around, but nobody I know has ever had tonsils out. Tiny Carlson had a broken arm set in the emergency room of Albany Hospital, but he couldn't tell me anything about the floors where operation patients go. Papa and Mama have never been inside a hospital, so they couldn't tell me much, either. Mama's biggest worry was having me ready on time Monday morning.

Sunday night she said, "Zach, I have packed with the pajamas one towel and one washcloth. Are you sure you know the street where the hospital is?"

"Of course he does. Straight through Washington Park and two blocks up the hill. Zach is a smart boy. Just remember to leave the house by eight o'clock," said Papa in a hearty voice.

Papa was going to report first to his boss at the port. Then he planned to catch a bus right after that and come uptown in time to meet me at the hospital.

Was it my imagination? Or did they both sound nervous?

The truth is I wasn't all that confident myself about the whole business. Monday morning didn't improve my condition. It was one of those gray-as-dust days, and I wondered if that was an omen. All Greeks believe in signs. The doctor said no breakfast before the operation. Having an empty stomach didn't help my queasy feeling.

It was a short walk to the hospital. Really short. I got there early. The admissions lady sat at a desk just inside the front door, and I told her my name and why I was there. From the way she looked around me and over me, I figured she meant to send me home. Quickly I said, "My father's coming up from work. He'll be here soon."

The lady still looked doubtful. "There are papers to fill out first. If he's late getting here . . . You're due to go upstairs by . . ." She shuffled her papers, looking for the time of the operation.

Dumb lady. Didn't it occur to her that if she was so worried about her schedule, I could fill out the forms? "Please, ma'am, to save time, let me do them."

She looked shocked. "I can't let you do that. You're underage. You can't sign yourself into the hospital. Your father has to sign the papers."

This fusspot lady who didn't listen was making a bad morning worse. With exaggerated politeness, I said, "You're absolutely 100 percent correct, ma'am. Still, just in case my father misses the first bus up, could I maybe fill in the name, address, and stuff like that? It'll keep us and you from getting behind."

Edging the blank form around a little, I read it by turning my head sideways. Just as I thought. It made more sense for me to do it myself since I know my own medical history better than anybody.

I coaxed her again, saying, "I print very clearly because, you see, my parents come from Greece and the Greek alphabet is very different." I added hastily, "Even though they write mostly Greek, Papa knows how to sign his name in English."

The phone on the desk rang. The woman waved at something behind me and said, "I can't concentrate with you talking at me. The writing table has pen and ink on it. If you're sure he's coming, you can make a start, I guess."

I think she caved in more because she wanted to get rid of me than because she was convinced by my speech. Anyway, I filled it all out. Except for the signature, of course. Where it said "salary/income," I made a wild guess and put $5,000 per year.

Waiting is bad. It gives you a chance to imagine things. John Talbot must know a lot about hospitals. Too bad I didn't think to talk with him. I screwed my head around to see the big round clock on the wall. Buses go every fifteen minutes. Papa should have been here by now. I couldn't . . . I wouldn't go home, then come back another day to wait all over again. But Papa must be on his way so that wasn't going to happen.

It's hard to kill time when you don't have a book to read or anybody to talk to. Lightly, I sketched Papa's first name on the signature line, making the *A* pointy the way he does. Then I dipped the pen in the inkwell and started a light drawing of the *P* in *Poulos*. I'd have it all set up and ready for him to go over.

Suddenly, the loudspeaker on the column behind me squeaked, buzzed, and squawked. The noise took me so much by surprise that I wrote out *Poulos* clearly and without thinking, just as I do when signing for myself. What the heck. Shrugging, I rewrote *Athanasius*, making it match *Poulos*. That desk lady would just have to give me a new form for Papa's signature, and I'd keep this copy for myself, like a souvenir.

The loudspeaker squawked again. "Mr. Poolss. Mr. Jack Athenzzus Poles, please report to Admissions."

I'm used to hearing my name mangled, so I hurried over to the desk. A different lady sat there. This one did three things at once: talked on the phone wedged between her shoulder and chin, wrote a note on a pad, and with her other hand reached across the desk to pluck the form out of my fingers. I tried to explain about needing a new copy, but this human speed machine didn't give me a chance.

She spit out questions at me, *rat-a-tat-tat* like a machine gun. "Are you the patient? Where's your father? Why aren't you upstairs?" A quick look at the form, then, "Did your father go to the men's room? Never mind. Here's Nurse, who will take you up. Your father can find you later."

A large hairy hand landed on my shoulder, and I twisted around to see the nurse. "Nurse" turned out to be a huge man with bristly red hair and a freckled face. I never before heard of a man working as a nurse, and suddenly I had this giant one to take care of me.

"Wait, we can't go yet," I said to the nurse, who with a hand on my back was moving me gently but firmly forward. I felt the way I do when I eat too much too fast.

"Nothing to be afraid of," he said, steering me into the elevator. "I had my tonsils out when I was your age, and you can see it didn't affect my growth one bit. Ha ha ha."

I had to tell him that the signature of Athanasius T. Poulos was not really by Papa, that in fact, Papa hadn't even arrived. I took a shaky breath and started. "Papa's not . . ."

"He'll be right there in the visitor's lounge when you wake up after the operation."

Lordy, I'd forgotten that they were going to give me gas. Was it legal to do that if Papa hadn't signed the form? I had so many things to worry about now that I didn't know where to start. Like how exactly were they going to do this operation? How were they going to reach all the way back to cut my tonsils out? And speaking of cutting, did they stick a *real knife* down my throat?

Where was Papa?

"Everything off. Put on the hospital gown that's on the chair and hop up on the bed," said the nurse. "I'll be back in a flash."

He'd led me to a bare little room after we got off the elevator. Beside the stretcher bed, there was a footstool and a chair. That was all. No machines, no equipment of any kind. I decided to do as I was told for the time being. Probably the doctor had to examine me again, but I was sure he couldn't do any cutting up until after Papa came.

Mama had insisted I put on clean underwear today. Even so, I hid it neatly inside my shirt and pants before putting the bundle on the chair. That stretcher bed was high. I used the footstool to half-climb, half-jump up onto it.

The nurse, who just came in, gave a hearty ho-ho and said, "Lie back, close your eyes, and get set for the thrill ride of a lifetime."

Automatically, I closed my eyes before I realized that the nurse hadn't made any sense. Just then the whole bed with me on it went shooting out the door. "Hey, you didn't tell me this bed has wheels. Hey, wait . . . where we . . . ?"

I tried to sit up, but the giant's big hand held me flatter than a tipped-over tombstone. Rolling down the hall, we picked up speed and barreled through some swinging doors into a brightly lit room. It was worse than being at a movie where the reel slips and the film runs at double time.

Bright, bright lights. It was the brightest room I've ever seen. And full of shiny metal machines and trays with corners and edges that caught the light and multiplied it. The room was cold, too, the coldest room I've been in all summer. If all the people in the room weren't wearing masks, I swear you'd be able to see their breaths. That's when I made up my mind. One thing I'll never be when I grow up is a doctor.

From the doorway, the red-haired nurse said, "Ta-ta. See you later, alligator."

A masked figure bent over and buckled a strap around my chest.

Clearly, my guardian angel was off duty today. With or without Papa's signature, I was about to have my tonsils taken out. I couldn't help thinking that Mama, who says I jump too quickly into things, should meet these hospital people. These guys were real champions compared to me. I hoped that at least they would take the right part out.

Another masked figure leaned over and spoke in a soothing voice. I couldn't concentrate so I can't tell you what it said, only that it was a man's voice. A cone slipped over my nose and mouth.

The last clear thought I had was of being mad . . . at myself. If I hadn't talked that woman into giving me a form . . . if I hadn't played with the form, I wouldn't be here yet. I, Zachary Athanasius Poulos, and my own big mouth were to blame.

It's a pity I can't put out of my mind forever what came after. Waking up was a gross experience. Two big black bats swam across my line of sight. I screamed, but as in a dream not a sound came out of my throat. Instead, I started to gag because swallowing was suddenly the most painful work in the world. I didn't remember that I was in a hospital, I didn't understand any of it. That's why, I guess, I was happy to see a familiar face.

"Coming to?" My friend, the nurse, cranked up the bed, tugged me and my pillow higher, and said, "Suck on this straw. Get some ice water down, and then I'll give you a real treat."

I shuddered. I remembered too clearly now the last treat: that thrilling ride down the hall into the operating room. By closing my eyes I made him go away.

The black bats were there again when I opened my eyes. Giant black bats about five feet tall whisked out of sight into the room across the way. Think, I told myself. For what reason would black bats fly around in a hospital? Maybe the hospital was doing vampire research?

When I saw a little white ghost stop in my doorway, I knew for sure that the ether had permanently damaged my brain. I squeezed my eyes shut tight. Unfortunately, my ears were still open.

"Zachary . . . Zachary . . ."

It was the tiniest whisper, but there was no mistake. The ghost was calling my name. Another tiny sound, a scampering like little mice feet, and again I heard "Zachary . . . Zachary," now from the other side of my bed. Maybe I had already died and only *thought* I was in the hospital?

I groaned, and that sound came out loud and real

enough to me. Somebody else heard it, too, because I got an answer from the hall.

A woman's voice called out, "Sure, and our Lord loves little children. Don't worry. You're in our prayers."

My eyes flew open, and I saw those two black bats walking out into the hall again, only now they looked more like penguins wearing big silver crosses. I blinked and realized that my penguin bats were nuns wearing black habits. With a cheery wave at me, the two were gone again.

Turning my head to the other side, I saw the little white ghost at my side. Only, the ghost had turned into Zoe wearing her white Sunday school dress.

"Zach, you never kissed me good-bye this morning," said Zoe, her big black eyes both accusing and sad at the same time. "I called and called you when I woke up, but you were gone. You're not s'pose to go . . . *zap* . . . away like that."

When I didn't say anything in answer, she looked worried. She leaned forward and poked my side with her finger, "Zach," her voice rose shrilly. "Zach, *say something.*"

Poor Zoe. I often get mad at her, but I don't really like to hurt her feelings or to scare her. I forced myself to whisper as loudly as I could. "I . . . hurt. . . ."

"Oh." A relieved look spread across her face. "I can help that." Stretching up and across the edge of the bed and tugging my shoulder toward her, she planted a wet kiss on the side of my neck. "Pretty soon you'll feel all better," she said confidently.

If it didn't hurt so much, I'd have laughed at Zoe's kissing my boo-boo to make it better. The best I could do was stretch my mouth a little in a weak smile.

Encouraged, Zoe said, "Watch the show, Zach." Her white dress looked like a fluttering sail as she did two rapid flips in a row. She came right-side up, grinning, and said, "I'm ready for the 'lympics whenever you say we can have them. Doesn't that make you feel better?"

I was in no shape to decide that, but I wondered aloud, "How . . . you . . . Papa?"

"Isn't Papa here already? No, I came all alone by myself," she said proudly.

Curiosity pushed me to try again. ". . . find hosp . . ."

"I did like you do. I went to the library. Miss Hastings made me a map. She said when I felt bad to look at the map and see how close you were and not to worry because you'd be home tomorrow or the next day. So I looked and I came," she finished triumphantly.

She added, "Oops, I almost forgot. Look." She held up a string bag with three books. "Miss Hastings picked them out, and they're all for a boy. Not one for me."

Putting the bag down on the floor, she squatted

and burrowed into it. "Wait'll you see what I got."

If I ever wondered how Zoe felt about me, she had just told me. Zoe's most valuable possession in the whole world is her library card. I've never been able to persuade her to take books out for me on her card when I want more than the three that we're allowed.

Right after that shock of discovery, a second one came along. A man's voice called, "*Zaharia, Zaharia*, I found you." The voice was Papa's, in fact, but I didn't recognize the man in the doorway. The guy standing there wore a white turban on his head. "You all right, my boy?"

I nodded weakly.

Papa moved quickly to my bedside. Close up, the turban turned into a big bandage wrapped around his head. He leaned over and kissed me on the forehead, murmuring, "Thanks be to God." Straightening, he said, "You must tell me—when you can talk comfortably—how it happened that you are operated on without a father or a mother present."

He was right. I needed time to find the right words. To say that I myself had made it happen sounded too stupid. I pointed to his bandage.

Papa answered the unspoken question. "That's why I wasn't here. A bundle of beams that were being unloaded from a ship broke apart. One falling grazed my head and knocked me out. If I had been conscious, I would tell them to bring me here. Instead the ambulance took me to Memorial Hospital, so we lost one another."

Zoe, who had popped up with a book in each hand, finally found her voice. "Does it hurt, Papa?"

Papa's face looked as if another beam had landed on his head. "*Zoe!* Where did you come from? What are you doing here?"

"I'm helping the way you always say we should," she replied. "I'm cheering up Zach."

"Children under fourteen are not allowed in the hospital. How did you get in?"

"I came in the door that was fixed open for the laundryman." She got sidetracked. "Children can so come. Zach's here, isn't he? And a lady in white brought me up to this floor 'cause she said all the children belong on this floor."

The nurse or whoever must have thought Zoe was an escapee from the children's ward.

Papa's tanned face had a deep red tinge as if he'd been out in the sun too long. He clenched his fists, then opened his mouth finally to ask, "And you left our neighborhood, you crossed all those streets by yourself? Mama does not know you are here?"

"You always tell me not to bother Mama at rush hour, and I didn't." Zoe tried out a smile and cocked her head as if waiting for praise. But she shifted her feet uneasily.

"She meant well," I whispered.

"Good intentions do not excuse bad actions. I

promise that is a lesson Zoe will learn today, never to forget again," Papa said grimly. "I will come back for a visit with you, Zach, after. After I take Zoe home and we have our talk."

I was glad it wasn't me that Papa was dragging out the door. Papa doesn't often make promises. When he does, it's always a promise that he knows—and I know—he can keep.

The nurse, who passed Papa and Zoe on their way out, was carrying something on a plate. He asked, "Ready for your treat?"

I eyed the plate suspiciously. I didn't trust his sense of humor one bit, so when he unwrapped my treat, it was another shock. Sitting bare and open was a double-stick orange Popsicle!

"Every four hours you get a Popsicle. Grape, next time," he said, leaving.

Well, this was more like it. In a way, I was having a double treat. I didn't have to share my Popsicles with Zoe, and for once she was going to get a fair share of one of Papa's lectures. You might even say I was getting my birthday presents early this year.

4

The Secret Weapon

I need to know. Once your body starts changing, does it ever stop halfway? I mean, leaving you like a freak halfway between being a kid and a grown-up? There must be a book that explains it all, but I know the librarian would say something if I found one and took it out. I need to know because I think maybe I've stopped. My nose looks bigger to me, but I'm not any taller.

My best bet for getting an answer, I think, is to ask John Talbot, who's been to college. Maybe he himself asked somebody that same question when he was my age.

As soon as I reached that decision, I felt better. But John hadn't come to the little park today, so my question had to wait.

"It's funny how one thing leads to another," said Abe in his loud quacky voice. Abe and I sat as usual on the steps of the monument to the Spanish-American War.

"Funny is the wrong word," I said, checking first

to see if anybody was within hearing distance. Only Abe knew about this other problem I have, and I didn't want the others to get wise. If I hadn't had a sore throat, if I hadn't had my tonsils out, I wouldn't be in this position. I still don't understand how Mama could do it to me. I thought she loved me. She says she does.

Louie, who was lying on the grass, called out, "Hey, Zach, what time we going to practice at Lincoln pool today?"

His question was the one I've been trying to avoid. No use ducking. I said, "Louie, you're on your own when it comes to swimming. I'm finished with going to Lincoln pool."

"You think you already can beat us all?" asked Louie.

I shrugged modestly.

"I don't believe it," said Patty, who'd come around the statue from the boulevard side. Her eyes narrowed suspiciously.

"Believe it or not," I declared, "I'm not going to Lincoln anymore. But don't let that stop those of you who need to polish up your strokes. See y' guys." I stood up, stretched, and headed back to the store and my own backyard before they asked too many questions.

No matter how much I exercise my brain there's no getting around the ugly truth. I *can't* go to Lincoln anymore, Mama says. According to her, it's the doctor who decided, but I'm not convinced. He told her the chances of getting an infection and especially polio are riskier right after an operation. Zoe, who's still got her tonsils, is allowed to go because, Mama says, lessons and learning are important.

It's no use sneaking off without permission. If Zoe doesn't squeal on me, somebody—a customer or George the peanut man—will surely come in the store and mention they saw me at the pool. That's no maybe either. Last Halloween when we smeared soap on store windows on Pearl Street all the way downtown, Frank the barber from uptown on Central saw me and told Papa.

When I want to cool off, I'm supposed to turn on the garden hose in the backyard! Depressing. The more I think about it, the more I get mad instead of sad. It's my body. Why didn't they let *me* decide whether I wanted to live with my bad tonsils? Or at least when to take them out. Probably, they were afraid I'd choose to do it after Labor Day when school starts.

Zoe, who'd followed me out to the yard, asked, "Zach, could you tie a hole in the end of my rope like the cowboys have?" She held out a long skinny piece of string.

"Tie a hole?" Zoe was making less sense than usual. Then the light dawned on me. "You mean you want a lasso?"

"Is that what you call it? Yes. What's it called in Greek?"

"Zoe, you're being a major moron. Cowboys are American. There isn't any Greek word for it," I replied. Or none that I knew, but I admitted that only to myself.

"Oh, yes there is. Because I told Mama and she's writing to our grandma *yiayia* that I want to be a cowgirl when I grow up," Zoe replied stubbornly.

I've explained to Zoe that *yiayia* means grandma, so she should use one or the other, but Zoe keeps on using both. I grinned, and taking the string from her said, "Seems like a poor career choice to me."

"What's that mean?" Zoe asked.

"Zoe, you're too scared to pat the Freihofer Bakery wagon horse when he stops at the water trough. A cowgirl gets lots closer than that to a horse. She gets on and rides it," I said.

That stumped her, I could tell. Meanwhile, I was stumped on how to tie a sliding noose, which is what a lasso is.

A crafty look came over Zoe's face. "That's because I'm still too little. And I will when Mama says I can . . . and the horse is my size."

"You need a heavy rope, Zoe. String won't work." I gave the string back to her.

Zoe might be willing to wait for Mama's permission, but I'm tired of having to do that. Zoe and I are *not* the same age. The question is: Will Mama ever stop lumping us together like identical twins and listen, really listen when I talk?

Abe understood the question was serious when I put it to him the next afternoon.

"My mother started treating me like I was older after my sister . . ." Abe stopped.

That's when I remembered. Abe's older sister had died from an infection because there weren't any medicines or doctors on the boat to Cuba. I was sorry I'd brought the subject up, but I had to point out, "I'm already the oldest."

"You need somebody to argue your case with your mother."

Raising an eyebrow, I looked at Abe and asked, "Are you volunteering?"

"Nah, you know better than that, Zach. If it comes out of a kid's mouth, grown-ups automatically ignore it."

"You're right. I'm just desperate," I said gloomily.

Abe left to go swimming with Patty Aylward. I didn't blame him. If I were Abe, that's what I'd do, too.

I don't have to worry about filling up time now that swimming is out. Mama kindly took care of that for me, too. She offered my services to Lalou, the old Greek man who owns the shoeshine stand in the New York State Office Building. He can't read or write. Not Greek and not English, so I go read his mail and write his letters for him.

Ever since the Nazis occupied Greece, Mama writes half a dozen letters every single week to her mother, our *yiayia*, and to all the other relatives. I do the same for old Lalou. Mama figures maybe one letter at least will get through. The Red Cross, which is helping, says it takes time, but we haven't heard any news in ten months.

Coming back from my four o'clock trip to the post office, I saw the kids up on the next block by the toy store. "Wait up," I yelled, and sprinted across the street. Only Abe and Zoe were missing from the crowd around Wylie Bowen. Everybody was listening with both ears to Wylie.

"I'm telling you there's no risk. Easier than falling off a log. I do it all the time," said Wylie. Nodding at Patty, he added, "Comes in handy when you want to give a special friend a little present."

Patty, who was studying something in her hand, had a funny look on her face. I couldn't tell if she was happy or not.

"Whatcha got?" I asked.

She held the "present" up for me to see. A key chain hung from a little red wooden shoe that had SOUVENIR OF ALBANY, NEW YORK painted on the side. It was a Dutch-style shoe because the Dutch came here to trade with the Indians way back. I read a lot of history books, so I can even tell you the date Albany got settled: 1624.

The shoe was cute, and I guess it's the thought that counts but still . . . a key chain for a present? Hardly anybody in our neighborhood ever locks doors.

"I don't get it," I said.

"You don't get a lot of things, Zach," said Wylie. It sounded awfully close to a sneer the way he said it.

Too bad Abe wasn't here. The way this scene was shaping up, I had the feeling I could use some reinforcements.

"What do you mean?" I asked Wylie.

Wylie answered, "I said what I mean. You don't get a lot of things. Just for instance, look at you and money. Who else is so stupid as to put in four and five hours of work a day for no pay?"

"You're the stupid, Wylie, not me, and I can prove it. Lemme ask you a question: Say you have a dime in your left-hand pocket. Then you move that dime over to your right-hand pocket. How much money have you got now?"

Wylie Bowen's round blue eyes blinked as he looked for the catch to the question. That's the other thing about Wylie that gets me. He has this round face with round eyes that he keeps wide open all the time. Nobody can be as innocent as Wylie Bowen looks.

"Ten cents. That's all you've got. Right?" Wylie looked around to see who agreed.

I nodded my head in agreement. "Correct. Absolutely. And that's what happens if I ask my pa for pay. I don't end up with any more money because *all* of the money my family makes is mine, too."

"I still don't see you jingling any good old do-re-mi in your pocket. So what can you buy for a friend?" Wylie said. It was one of those questions that's not asking but telling.

Score one for him. I was trying to think of an answer when he turned away. Over his shoulder, he said, "Who wants to have some fun and get some goodies? Follow me, and I'll show you how."

A big smile crossed Mousie's face. He said, "Me," and bumped Tiny out of his way.

"Me . . . Me . . . I want . . . I'm coming with you, Wylie, boy . . ."

The whole crowd took off racing and whooping behind Wylie. From where I stood, they reminded me of a pack of dogs. I'm used to being up in front of the kids, not trailing along at the rear. But if I wanted to learn who got what and where they were getting it, I'd have to follow along with the rest of them.

"You'd think he promised them something for nothing or a pot of gold," I said to Patty. She had waited at the corner of Lexington for me.

"He did," she said.

87

"Yeah? Which one of the two did he promise?" I asked.

"Both," said Patty.

I started to say, "I don't get it," then shut my mouth. I settled instead for working out a comeback to Wylie's last remark and had it by the time we caught up.

Everybody had braked and settled in front of Woolworth's. A couple of kids sat on the fender of a car parked at the curb; one was leaning against the lamppost. I stopped at the fireplug ten feet away and said, "I don't need dough because I don't have to *buy people* to be my friends."

Wylie's round eyes almost looked narrow as he answered. "You missed the beginning, Zach-o. I don't *buy* anything. All that stuff on the counters . . ." He nodded toward Woolworth's. "Well, some of it's special, marked, and free for you and me."

How did Wylie know that? I never heard of such a thing. Of course, he's been around more than us. Maybe he had a relative working there who knew when the company wanted to dump stuff, and how it was done.

Just thinking about stuff in the five-and-ten reminded me of a wallet in Woolworth's that I had my eye on. In my head I even caught a whiff of the special smell that brand-new leather has. I hope to get that wallet in brown by Christmas. Twice already I've told Papa how dangerous it is to carry money loose in your pants pocket.

"If they're giving stuff away, I know what I want," I told Wylie. "But you said it's marked. How? And whadda you have to do to get it?"

"Anything you eyeball is 'marked.' You just free it up from the counter." Wylie gave a quick lifting motion and then slid his hand into his pocket.

Everybody laughed, but I shivered. Maybe I don't always get it, but I could feel in my bones that a disaster was coming. For the record, my bones have only been wrong once.

"So far, I've freed up a couple of address books, some spools of thread, a lipstick, even an alarm clock. And I can't tell you how many key chains I've picked up," Wylie bragged.

"Junk. Who wants that junk anyway?" I said.

It's not that I never in my life took something that didn't belong to me. I used to raid a convent garden to snitch pears from the trees. And not mentioning names, you understand, but every kid I know has taken pennies from his mother's pocketbook at least once. This was different, somehow.

Wylie ignored me. "The trick is to spread out along a counter with everybody asking to see different things all at the same time. That keeps the sales clerk busy and dizzy. She doesn't have time to notice when a guy at the other end pockets something."

"Yeah, and when the floorwalker comes along and puts the arm on you, then what?" I argued.

The kids moved kind of restlessly, and somebody mumbled, "Zach is right. The floorwalker will get you. That's his job."

"I already scouted out the enemy, and I guarantee that Shapiro will be snoozing in his office," said Wylie.

I didn't believe him. I wished again that Abe Zalkin had shown up. Between the two of us, we might—maybe—talk the kids out of going in there.

"Who wants to free up some goodies? Who's going to be first to enlist? Wylie looked around the crowd in a challenging way.

He made it sound like some kind of war game between us and Woolworth. Mousie's eyes were shining with excitement. Even Louie got caught up in the spirit.

"This is not shaping up like our usual boring summer," said Louie. That was a real storm of words coming from him.

"Maybe one of us should be a decoy? Go up to Shapiro with a complaint or something if he comes out of his office. That would stop him," offered Tiny, but he sounded doubtful.

"What's a dee-coy? You guys playing a new game? Let me in, too," said Zoe's voice beind me. I groaned. This mess was bad enough without having to worry about Zoe.

"Hey, Wylie, Zoe can be our decoy. She can pretend she's lost her mother," said Mousie excitedly.

I saw a big beaming smile spread across Zoe's face. Except for Patty and Abe, most of my friends treat Zoe like a pesty little kid. Usually they try to shut her out of what's going on. To be invited in was a rare treat for her.

"Zoe only does what I allow her to do," I reminded them all in a sharp voice. Today was a topsy-turvy day with Wylie pulling everybody along. But no matter what kind of day it is, I'm always in charge of Zoe.

"No, I'm the boss of me," Zoe declared. "How come you don't want Mr. Shapiro to walk around? Doesn't he have to say you can take what you want?"

"Forget her," Wylie directed. "You guys take the side next to the candy counter and spread out."

"Where are you gonna be, Wylie?" asked Tiny.

"Oh, I'll take the far side from all of you, over by the passport pictures booth. Or I'll roam up and down," he answered looking away from Tiny. "Remember, we go half-and-half on everything you lift, so pick up as much as you can. Woolworth's is rich. They'll never miss what we take."

I've heard that line before. There are kids who think *I'm* rich because we've got a whole cooler full of sodas in the store. Those are the kids who think I ought to pass free sodas around every day.

Now, I tried. I explained to Wylie and the rest of

them the way Papa had explained it all to me when I took Dentyne gum packs from our store without asking. I told them how no store gets something for nothing. The owner has to buy it from somebody else to begin with.

"And when stuff doesn't sell or gets stolen, the five-and-ten has to charge more on other stuff to make a profit. You don't really get something for nothing. In fact, pretty soon your notebooks, pencils—*what you really need and have to buy will cost you more.* So you lose in the end," I warned them.

"Are you finished, Mister Professor Poulos?" asked Wylie with a sneer. "Anybody who's chicken—or babies like Zoe—can stay outside with mother-hen Zach. The rest of you, forward march."

Louie wouldn't look at me. Tiny gave a little shrug and drifted closer to Louie. Patty gave me a begging look I couldn't figure before she started after Tiny. All the kids began going through Woolworth's door by twos and singly.

My blood boiled. Wylie had made it just about impossible for anyone to stay out of it. Not me, though. I don't have to prove anything to a Wylie Bowen. No, siree. He never did walk the top railing on the viaduct like Tiny or spend a night hiding from Nazis in a foreign country like Abe. Not to mention stopping crooks from robbbing your best friend's father like I did in Cohoes when we lived there.

I called after Wylie, who was actually the last one going in. "You're not freeing anything. In plain English, Wylie, you're stealing. *If* and *when* I ever go to jail, it will be for a better reason than a junky key chain."

The decision not to go still felt right. But I felt awful. I had no doubt in my mind or bones that they all were going to get caught. Somehow I felt I was to blame. If only I had been able to think of a better game . . . if I had talked faster. . .

"How come you didn't make them stay, Zach?" Zoe asked, making me feel worse.

"For cryin' out loud, Zoe, you heard me. I practically talked my tonsils out," I said.

"You mean they grew back already? I didn't know they could do that," Zoe said, looking curiously at my mouth. Then, without waiting for an answer, she turned away from me.

"Wait . . . where are you going? Come back here, Zoe."

Zoe, eyes wide and worried, looked back over her shoulder. "Patty is one of us. Remember the Musket Ears' rule? All for one and one for all."

Zoe never says the name quite right—she always splits it into two words. But she sure has the motto down pat. And, boy, she takes being a Musketeer very seriously.

"We gotta rescue Patty. We gotta help even if it

kills us," said Zoe. Once again she started for the entrance to Woolworth's.

I hauled her back by the straps of her sunsuit. I don't know if a rescue would kill us, but I'd sooner serenade crocodiles than face Papa if Zoe got caught with shoplifters. I scowled at Zoe.

"This is no game."

"I know. And that's why you're gonna save Patty from jail, right?" Zoe said. When Zoe sets her mind or heart on something, she is mule-stubborn about getting it. Now she stood and waited, her big black eyes positive that I could pull it off.

What could I do? Friends don't squeal on friends, so I wasn't about to knock on Shapiro's door and get him after the kids. But I'm sorry to say, Zoe was right. I couldn't just walk away, either.

"Zoe, only a magician could make this come out right, and I don't know any magic tricks."

All I know how to do, Mama says, is talk. She claims I have the biggest mouth in the world and more words than there are weeds. Think. I had to think, but it was hard to start. My head seemed to be stuffed with buzzing bees.

Magicians pull their tricks by turning your attention away from what they're really doing. Magic. Bees. The two words came together in my head with a clash, and I saw a spark of light in a corner of my brain.

Oh, okay. I had a plan—not great—but a plan of

94

sorts. First, Zoe had to be stashed somewhere safe. Telling her to stay out of it wouldn't do any good. That was like telling water not to be wet. She'd never wait patiently outside.

Then I got inspired. "Zoe, this is like a war between Wylie and me, and guess what? You're going to be my secret weapon." I chuckled as if I were giving her the best part.

"Do I have to hide?" asked Zoe, interested but puzzled.

Good. Her mind was working just the way I wanted it to.

"Sort of. I go in first, see. Then you come in and settle by the magazine rack in the corner where the door to Shapiro's office is. While you look through *Life* or one of the other magazines, I'll launch an attack to pull Patty away."

"What do I do to help, though? Be a lookout?"

"Yeah, that's it," I said, hastily crossing my fingers to excuse the lie. "Nobody will guess that we belong together. You watch out for Shapiro and warn me if he's coming."

At least part of what I said was true. Nobody connects the two of us because we look so different. Greeks at church who want to tease say I must be from Poland.

As for the rest of what I said, Zoe would be out of it long before anything happened. Anytime a kid sits and reads magazines, a clerk chases the kid away and *out of the store*. Outside she'd be safe from arrest.

Just then, too late to do any good, Abe Zalkin came strolling up the avenue. He gave us a lazy wave. Zoe waved back and yelled excitedly, "Hurry up, Abe, so you can join the war, too."

"Which war?" Abe called back. "Don't forget: in war you have to duck and run for cover." He always talks to Zoe straight, just as if they were the same age. "What's your hurry, Zach? Where's the fire?"

His words set off something like an explosion in my head. *Duck.* That's what Wylie was going to do. Duck in the photo booth and leave the other kids holding the bag—or the hot goods—if the clerks or Shapiro got wise to what was happening. That's why Wylie said he'd take the side of the counter away from the others.

" . . .that Wylie is a bigger rat than I dreamed."

From looking puzzled, Abe's face went to looking alarmed. "What are you saying? Do you mean what I think?" asked Abe.

I must have been doing my thinking out loud. I said grimly, "No time now. I'll explain better later. They've already been in there long enough to pocket things."

I raced into the store.

You couldn't miss them. More than ever, they reminded me of a pack of dogs. Yipping and yapping away, up and down the counter. Maybe it was just

96

my imagination, but it seemed like the clerk had the same picture in her head. She was showing Mousie the compartments in a wallet but she held it just out of his reach.

Circling the candy counter as if I couldn't decide what to buy, I looked across the aisles. Yep, there was Wylie on the far side of the other counter. He certainly was apart, and he acted as if he didn't know anybody in the noisy crowd.

Was I too late? Had something already been stolen? I tried to watch without seeming as if I were watching. I checked the photo booth. The curtain was pulled halfway across, but it must have been empty because there were no feet showing.

A glimmer up above caught my eye. An oddly curved mirror hung high on the wall above the photo booth. I'd never before noticed it. The way that mirror tipped out, it showed everybody and everything in a line up to the door of Shapiro's office.

I could see the kids, I saw Louie's hand reach out, then pull back . . . empty, thank goodness. I saw . . . and *so did Mr. Shapiro, who had come out of his office.* He was moving briskly forward. Suddenly Shapiro's head ducked down in a kind of nose-dive. I didn't wait to see if it came up again.

"Bees," I yelled at the top of my lungs. "Look out for the bumblebees."

I charged around the counter, slapping Louie and

Tiny hard against the shoulders. "Got one! I think. Look out! Here come more!"

"Bees," shrieked Patty. "I'm allergic to bees. Get out of my way or I'll throw up on you." And she went down the counter aisle like a whirlwind, scattering kids right and left.

Wow! Almost as if she knew what I wanted to happen. Patty was a great help. I charged down to the end and slapped at Mousie's hand so hard, he dropped the key chain.

"They're all over. Bees, bees," I kept on yelling.

Ding, ding, ding. Eeek. The salesclerk was ringing the "help" bell hard with one hand and with the other swatting to keep any bees away. The assistant manager, a stock boy, clerks—a whole mob started piling around the counter.

In all the uproar you could hardly hear yourself think. Still, I heard this creepy-sounding voice plainly. Wylie, who had darted toward the photo booth, must have heard it, too. It came from somewhere around or inside the empty booth.

"*Whooo?* Who knows what evil lurks in the heart of men? *The Shadow Knows.*"

What happened next was was *un*believable. Wylie—just like the crooks on the radio show—yelled, "Who said that?"

The Shadow is invisible, of course. And the Shadow always, always captures the crooks by the end of each program. But what was he doing in Woolworth's?

Eyes rolling wildly, Wylie turned back and headed toward the counter. He didn't get his pockets emptied before the assistant manager clamped a hand on his arm. No other kids were left by the counter. I let my breath out in a big whoosh of relief.

Omigosh. Zoe. Was *she* out?

Moving fast, I looped around the back of the store, then down the aisle toward the magazine section, keeping away from the crowd.

Good old secret weapon Zoe.

She had plunked herself down on a pile of magazines at the bottom of the rack. Her legs stuck straight out so she was a natural booby trap for anybody hurrying . . . like Mr. Shapiro. He hadn't yet finished dusting off the knees of his pants.

"Little girl," Shapiro said in an angry voice, "the way you had your feet out, you're lucky I didn't break a leg tripping over you."

Myself, I figured *he* was the lucky one not to get his leg broken. I guess you can't expect a whole lot of sense from a man who had just flattened his nose on the floor of his own store.

"What's your name? Where do you live? I'm going to take you straight home and tell your folks what you did. What's a little girl like you doing out all alone anyway?"

Zoe opened and closed her mouth again. She looked very very small. Captured. That was the only word to describe the scene.

Shapiro continued to scold. "Don't you know those magazines are for sale? They're not toys to play with, even if you like to pretend to read."

"*Pretend* . . . I . . . can so . . ." Zoe's pride had really been hurt. She was so mad she couldn't talk.

I prayed Zoe would stay mad . . . and speechless. At least then Shapiro would never learn her name or where we lived. If he showed up at our store with his story of damaged magazines and dirty pants, guess who would get the blame from Papa and Mama. My brain felt as if it had shrunk down to a pea. I hadn't had much of a plan in the first place, and I didn't have any ideas left for this emergency in the second place.

"All for one. Zach, keep moving." Abe's whisper floated back as he passed me and put himself between Shapiro and Zoe.

"She's learning, always learning more English yet," Abe said. He spoke slowly, hesitantly as if he wasn't sure of the words. Abe sounded like somebody who didn't know much English. "Magazines is good way to learn about America, yes, mister?"

Abe took Zoe's hand in his and smiled up at Shapiro as if certain he would understand. Shapiro looked down at Zoe's dark head, then at Abe's curly mop. His face softened.

"How long have you been in this country?" he asked.

"Two years already, but you know, still it's hard to . . ." Abe's voice trailed off, and he shrugged.

"You speak pretty good English. Don't worry, your little sister will learn fast. But tell her, the magazines aren't for . . ."

I told myself to concentrate on getting out the door. After that I could laugh out loud for as long as I wanted. Not one minute later Abe and Zoe came out grinning. The sight of us brought Patty out from behind the lamppost.

"Before Shapiro connects us with Wylie or changes his mind about letting us off easy, run," I said. "Run."

And we all four did. We never stopped until we got to the little park, where we collapsed at the base of the statue. No one else was in sight. All the other kids must have headed straight home and holed up.

"I didn't think you guys were ever going to make it out of there. Zach, you know I never ever would do what Wylie says. But I went in to see if there was any way I could help Tiny and Louie out," said Patty.

It must be that girls think alike. "You and Zoe, both. But you oughtta think things through first and work out a plan," I answered. "Abe, making yourself the invisible Shadow and that creepy voice was genius, pure genius. How did you . . . ?"

"Easy," Abe said smugly. "I held my nose while I talked and stood up on the seat in the booth so no feet showed. Good thing you talk to yourself out loud so I could work out what was going to happen. But, Zach, if you hadn't dreamed up those bees, I don't know . . ." And he shook his head.

We sat for a minute thinking about all of our friends maybe getting caught by the manager.

Looking very worried, Zoe asked, "Zach . . . Zachary, what I want to know is: Is Wylie a friend or not? I mean, how can I tell if we gotta count someone as friend?"

Good question. I sat up straight. Somehow my unconscious must have been working on this because the words came right out.

"A friend, Zoe, a true friend doesn't ask you to do something you know is wrong—like harming somebody else. And a real friend doesn't get you into a dangerous spot and leave you there."

"To do that is a true and mortal sin," Patty exclaimed.

Zoe's worried look disappeared. What a relief for me, too. I don't have to feel guilty about not liking Wylie Bowen.

Patty reached out and clapped her hand on my shoulder. She yelled, "Bees, bees. Bzzz."

Abe howled with laughter, and a second later I joined him. We both rolled, laughing, off the base of the statue and drummed our heels on the grass till the tears came. Patty kept "bzzzing," and in between she whooped with big gusty laughs. Only Zoe sat still, brooding and unsmiling.

Suddenly she spoke, "I *can so* read, and I'll prove it to that man. I'm going back to write my name and my address for him."

Uh-oh. Secret weapon Zoe had just turned herself into secret menace Zoe. To stop her, I'd have to pull out my other secret weapon: my great brain power. But just now, I couldn't stop laughing.

5
The Altar Boys' Strike

Zoe came trotting into the backyard carrying a skinny red book that I recognized as mine. Ordinarily I don't like her touching my stuff, but she's welcome to the book we use in Greek school for religious instruction. It's full of long hard words that nobody understands even after they've been explained.

Still feeling generous, I said, "You can have the table if you want. I'm just leaving."

Lying flat on the tabletop under the shade of the maple tree is the best way to read a book. I felt good all over because I'd finished my book, and soon the kids would be back from swimming. I had news to tell them about my friend John Talbot.

"No," Zoe said, full of importance. "This is not a lying-down book. I have to read sitting up to learn by heart."

"Zoe, you already know 'Our Father who art in Heaven.' You're way ahead of everybody in your class."

"It's not for class. It's just me that's going to say the *Pistevo* in church."

That's when I burst out laughing. If you know anything about the Greek church, you'd laugh, too. Zoe might learn all those jaw-breaking words, but she would never in a million years get to stand up and recite the prayer that's called the Creed. Only boys or men do that. Usually, one of us altar boys comes out from behind the altar to stand in front of the priest and read it.

"It doesn't work that way in Greek church, Zoe. In fact, you're lucky we let you girls sit downstairs with us in the real church."

I laughed again. Papa says in Vlasti, his old village, girls and young women stay up in a balcony hidden behind a screen; only old ladies are downstairs where the men are. Worse yet, there are no seats at all and everybody stands through the whole service.

Zoe was too pleased with herself to be bothered by what I said. Opening the book to page 34, she started sounding out: *"Pis-te-vo ees e-enan . . ."* When I left, her eyes and the book were closed as she tried to repeat the words without looking.

I had more effect on the guys in the park. Hearing my news, they erupted with shocked questions: "We gotta cancel?" "For how long . . . ?" "Why . . . ?"

I patted the letter in my pocket. It was written in block letters, not too shaky, but signed in cursive:

Your friend, John Talbot. "I don't know what to say," I said, shaking my head.

"A Zach who's speechless? Tell me it's not true," said Louie the Lip.

"Actually, it's a stroke of good luck," I said finally.

"Good luck that John Talbot has gone to Boston and we don't have anybody to run a swimming Olympics?" Tiny's voice said plainly I must be nuts.

Well, it was for me. Thanks to his leaving, I won't have to admit that I'm not allowed to go swimming. "From John's point of view," I explained. "He's been waiting a long time for the insurance company to pay for his accident. And you gotta be glad if that therapy in Boston Hospital helps him."

But nobody was feeling kind-hearted or noble. Louie gave me a mean grin and said, "Now you'll never know if you could have beat everybody."

Did I say I like to stick with my friends? It's complicated, more complicated than I told Zoe. I'm beginning to think I might be better off if some of us came unstuck. When a person does a man's work like I do, it matures his brain. So he can look to be friends with more, different kinds of people than just kids on the block. Like me and John Talbot.

Tiny grumbled, "There's nothing to do . . . unless . . . maybe . . . Before Wylie got sent away by his aunt, he told me where there's a free show. Stand on the stone wall behind Anna May's house around eleven tonight and we can't miss Anna May's mother."

"Why would I wantta see *her*?" I asked.

"Because when Anna May's mother comes home from the saloon, she takes all her clothes off in front of the window."

"Ugh," I said. "That's a lousy show." Anna May's mother has two chins, and she jiggles all over when she walks on her high heels.

Patty gave Tiny a disgusted look and said, "That makes you a Peeping Tom, which gets you arrested, y' know."

"Zach, you have to think of . . ." said Mousie.

"Uh-uh, Mousie. I'm not ever getting stuck again with finding something to do," I said. Across the street I spotted Mr. Berry's ice truck parking. "What I think is it's time to cool off. There's the ice wagon; I gotta go."

Everybody runs to hang around the back of the truck and beg or snitch chips of ice. Only for me the ice wagon means I go back to work at the store. It's my job to move the sodas in the cooler and make room for the new ice.

We're probably the only street in America whose iceman is an icelady. Mr. Berry drives the truck but his daughter Lucy carries the ice blocks into the stores. If you saw Lucy, you'd understand. That girl is almost six feet tall and has muscles. She wears a little leather cape tied around her neck to keep her shirt dry and when she heaves a fifty-pound block up on her shoulder, you'd think it was a marshmallow.

Today she came around the counter and slid the block off smooth and easy. When the tongs let go, the ice sank like a submarine.

"Hey, squirt, did your pants shrink in the flood? Or did you make up your mind to grow?" asked Lucy. Putting out her hand, she squeezed my arm muscle.

"Cripes, let go," I yelped. Frankenstein's bride couldn't have icier fingers.

Lucy laughed and tossed her thick black braid back over her shoulder. She rolled her eyes and said, "Wow. I definitely felt a mouse-sized muscle there."

"Let me see," said Steve, the Pigman, who came out of the kitchen with garbage pails in each hand. "I'm an expert on growing."

Steve's the farmer who collects garbage from us and other places to feed and fatten up his pigs. He wears overalls and high rubber boots even on the hottest summer days because pig pens are mucky. But on his days off, he gets all duded up and slicks down his wavy gold hair with smelly stuff.

Steve looked me over or pretended to. Actually, he kept sneaking looks at Lucy. "He's growing, all right. Why, you're almost big enough to take a girl on a date," he said, giving her a big wink. "You line anybody up yet for the Central Avenue Merchants' boat ride and picnic?"

"Huh?" Why did I have the feeling that more was being said than I heard?

"If you shop on Central Avenue, you get a ticket at half-price for a ride on the Dayliner steamboat and a picnic at Kingston. So, you interested?"

Once again Steve wasn't looking at me but at Lucy.

Lucy, who was already on her way out the door, said, "I like water, solid or liquid." Giggling and eyeing Steve's garbage truck double-parked in the street, she added, "But I do enough riding in trucks all week. I don't ride in them on my days off."

"Neither do I," said Steve. "That's why I bought me a Caddy." He was following so close on her heels that the pails almost banged the backs of her legs.

"Wait," I yelled. "How much are the tickets?"

"Seventy-five cents, kids under five, free," Steve called.

Boy! Seventy-five cents is a bargain. The steamboats that go all the way to New York City on the Hudson River are big enough to travel on an ocean. Fifty miles down the river at Kingston there is a park for picnics. The boat coming up the river from New York City would bring everybody back to Albany. None of us has ever made the trip, though

I've heard about it ever since we moved to Albany. When I told the kids after supper, they agreed it was the best deal to come up all summer.

"Everybody shops on the avenue, so getting the tickets is a snap," said Patty. "I wonder what you wear for a boat ride?"

"Clothes, dummy." Abe snickered.

I had more important things than clothes to think about. Zoe plus a boat the size of the Dayliner equals trouble. I had to find a way to leave her at home and a way to get a ticket.

At supper that night I told Papa and Mama about the picnic trip.

"I know," said Papa. "Joe next door has tickets. What do you say, Mama? You want to take a little holiday with the children?"

Mama closed her eyes and shuddered. Then opening them, she said, "Like yesterday I remember coming across that ocean. Fourteen days throwing up without stopping. Such a foolish question to ask me!"

Papa looked up at the ceiling and said, "I thought we should buy a couple of tickets to support our friends the merchants."

"Buy, if you must," said Mama. "But I don't use them. Nor Zach, nor Zoe."

"Why not? I'm old enough to go by myself. What do you mean we can't use them?" I asked after I got my breath back.

"Too dangerous," said Mama firmly. "You go on boats only to get across to somewhere, not to ride for a good time."

I don't like to say my mother is crazy, but what she said sure was crazy.

"Besides, the week after is the St. Markos picnic," Mama added. "You want a good time, we all go there."

Couldn't she see it wasn't the same thing? The St. Markos picnic is when all the Greeks in Albany who come from Vlasti go to a farm and cook lamb on spits over an open fire. I think they pretend they're back in the Old Country.

"That's where *your* friends go for a good time. *My* friends are going on the Dayliner, and I want to go where they're going." I didn't exactly yell, but Mama knew I was mad, all right.

She looked at me with one eyebrow raised. "All your friends go jump off a cliff, you going to jump, too?"

I got so boiling mad then that I did a dumb thing. I shouted, "Yes."

"That proves it. You're too young to know what is for your own good," Mama said, getting in the last word as I slammed out of the store.

It's not only missing the boat trip; it's the unfairness of her "no" that got me. How come I'm not too young to get up at five o'clock on Saturday mornings and go with Papa to the Farmers' Market?

Papa bargains to get the best prices on the tomatoes and onions we use to make our special sauce for the hot dogs. But I'm the one who loads the bushel baskets into the wagon. And I'm not too young to steady the baskets and push as Papa hauls the wagon up State Street hill. Zoe, of course, is sound asleep at home. It's just Papa and me.

Going to market this week, Papa used up all our time together explaining Mama's "no." "Zach, in Vlasti there are only little streams, no big water, no swimming pools. Few know how to swim. First and only time Mama got closely acquainted with water was on the boat trip to America. Besides worrying about the boat sinking, she was pregnant with you and sick."

"I don't believe she can still be afraid. She just doesn't want me to have any fun," I said, kicking a wheel on the wagon.

"Zach, I ask you: Would *you* forget quickly two whole weeks of throwing up? And she had no mother to help her, not even anybody speaking Greek except me," Papa said, and sighed.

Maybe he feels he has to keep trying to make it up to her. But that's no reason why I should have to give up my first chance to go sight-seeing someplace besides my own city.

"Papa, *I need* to go on the Dayliner."

"You *want* to go," Papa corrected me. Glancing

112

at me, he said, "*Zaharia*, please, let's not give Mama any more to worry about. She has enough worry waiting to hear if our family is living or has maybe been killed by the Nazis."

I could tell it was no use, but I had to say one more thing. "Me going—or not going—on the Dayliner won't take away her worry about the war in Greece."

Since Papa was no help, I lined up Abe. Just like we planned, in front of Mama he asked, "Zach, your ma making anything special for you to eat on the boat picnic?"

Mama's proud of being a good cook, and I figured she'd see the picnic as a chance to prove it. But she simply went on counting out change for Bud Fenner.

It was Bud who smiled and said, "Going down the Hudson River is beautiful. You even see a castle like on the Rhine River in Germany."

"How do you know what the Rhine's like?" Abe asked suspiciously.

"Because I saw it when I was a boy, before my family came here in 1908."

I was glad Bud mentioned what year his family came from Germany. I could see the same relief in Abe's eyes. If Bud's family has been in the United States that long, they can't be Nazi-lovers.

"It's historical, too. You're traveling on the same

river as the first steamboat in America," said Bud.

"So, you'd say it's an educational trip? You can learn a lot?" I asked loudly.

Abe took the hint right away. "Oh, that's why my mother is *making* me go. She says breathing that—um—river air is healthy, too."

Still Mama said not one word. I couldn't even tell if she heard us. She just sat down at the table in back and picked up the newspaper.

Later Abe said, "You know, Zach, since we don't understand how your mother can say no, maybe we should get a female to work on her?"

Patty tackled the job the very next day, after she and Zoe came back from Lincoln Park. First she told Mama that Zoe was the best Tadpole swimmer at Lincoln. Then she added, "But, you don't even have to be a good swimmer when you go on the Dayliner. The boat has thousands of life jackets stuffed in the ceiling over your head."

Darn Patty. She ought to know better. Behind Mama's back, I made a face, silently moving my lips to say, "No boat sinking talk, no Zoe."

"Huh?" Patty stared, but she's smart and she caught on fast. "Anyway, it's the *calmest* trip because the stores are hiring teachers to make the day go okay. Miss Lang, the sixth-grade teacher, is going to talk about the history and geography of the river. Don't you think all kids should go to hear Miss Lang?"

We both waited anxiously for Mama's answer.

Mama reached behind the cash register for a package of Dentyne gum. Ignoring Patty's question completely, she handed Patty the gum and said, "Your mama brought you up a good girl, Patty. Thank you for taking Zoe to the lessons."

"Thanks, Mrs. Poulos." Patty's shrug admitted that she had butted against a stone wall. "See ya, Zach."

"Fos ek foton, thaion, a-li-thinon. . . ."

Zoe, the thin red book in her hand again, walked between Mama and me. She wore a glazed look like a sleepwalker, as she headed for the backyard, muttering the Greek words to the Creed.

It's amazing how she's willing to torture herself learning the *Pistevo*, all to make a game more real. For one second, I wondered: Should I have enlisted Zoe to help? Mama's kind of soft when it comes to Zoe.

The screen door slammed again. I went automatically to wait on Henry from the Armory Garage next door. His order never changes, so I drew a mug of coffee from the big urn and put it with a jelly doughnut in front of him.

Henry bit into his doughnut, and powdered sugar flew all over. The white-sugar beard looked funny on his black chin. He shook his head in mock disgust. "Did you put disappearing jelly in this one? Where's the princess? She always finds a fat one with lots of real jelly for me."

Henry kids a lot. Once he joked to Zoe that he needed a daughter and suggested that she should marry his son. Zoe told me later she didn't want to hurt Henry's feelings by reminding him that he wasn't a Greek. So she told him instead that she planned to marry a prince.

Today Henry, nodding at the half-circle of snapshots above the doughnut jar, said, "That dictator Mussolini still has his boots in your grandma's yard. Any day your picture will be going up there, too."

Some of our customers have been drafted, even though the United States hasn't declared war on anybody yet; some, like Bobby Paulus, went up to Canada and enlisted. So far, eight guys have given us snaps of themselves in their army uniforms to put up on the wall until they come back.

"No! The Allies will chase Italians and Germans out of Greece long before Zach is old enough to put on uniforms." Mama, who was filling the napkin holders, contradicted Henry sharply.

For once Henry looked serious. "Sure hope it's quick. Did you know that with a parent's consent, boys of seventeen can enlist and fight?"

"Please don't give Zach any ideas. Besides, he's too, too young, only now turned thirteen," she said.

"Down south where I come from, thirteen is close enough to being a man. A kid that age can pick a lot of cotton. I sure had to." Then Henry added, "Seems to me Zach does as much here as any man."

His last words sure sounded good to my ears, but Mama looked startled by what he said.

"Maybe so, but Zach is not an age for joining in armies. No," Mama repeated. Then she cocked her head the way she does when she's thinking. "Still, you're right. He does and can do a lot, more even than I think sometimes."

My heart leaped into my throat. I could feel it beating like a bird trying to get free. If she felt that way . . . now while her guard was down, maybe I could win her over?

Mama did reach a decision. She announced, "You're old enough, Zach. Tomorrow after supper Papa will teach you how to chop onions and how to make the sauce."

Zoe's the lucky one in our family. At her age she can cry when her hopes come crashing down. I didn't cry, of course, but all night long, snaky thoughts slid in and out of my head. By the time Papa and I started steaming the tomatoes and chopping onions, I was set to attack again.

I began cautiously. "Pop, would you say I'm an American kid?"

"Of course, you're born here in America. What else could you be?"

"And didn't you say that we should know what

else is going on around us in this world?" I asked as I slid the skin off a boiling hot tomato that I had fished out of the kettle.

Papa looked up from the mountain of onions he was peeling. "These questions, Zach, have a reason? You're not just filling the air with sound?"

"What kind of American can I be, Papa, if I don't ever see any other parts of the country?"

The only sound I heard was Papa's knife thumping steadily through the onions onto the wooden chopping block.

"Papa? Are you thinking about what I said?"

"It's the question of the Dayliner again, yes? Here. Try it. Hold the knife so your thumb steadies the blade as it goes up and down."

"I know you think I want to go just because everybody else is. But I truly *need* to go so I can learn American ways. You and Mama grew up Greek, so you can't tell me those things." Onion bits flew all over the chopping block as I slammed the knife down hard.

"Zach, use your blade to shove the pieces into a pile. When you have to chop a bushel of onions, you must save energy and motion."

Here I am fighting for my future in America, and Papa's mind was on onions! It's enough to make even a strong man cry. Papa, in fact, was crying, but not over my situation. His tears were from onion juice perfuming the air.

"Can't you see how already my life is different from yours and Mama's? Why, I can swim out to the raft at Lincoln."

"True. You're ahead of me, too, Zach, because you'll know how to chop onions. A skill I didn't learn until I was a grown man in America."

I had to get him back to the main point. Which is that Mama's own history from long ago and her ideas about Greek boys are keeping me from living like a real and regular American boy.

Papa continued, "How lucky you are to have *two* worlds to draw from. Look how from the Greeks you got a gift for using words, and from America, free education and lots of opportunity to use your words. Maybe you'll grow up to be a rich lawyer."

A lawyer? I like the idea of making money just by using words. But then I had a gloomy thought, and I said, "What gift for words? I sure can't convince Mama to change her mind. I'd probably end up a poor and hungry lawyer."

Papa had lifted the towel tucked in his apron strings up over his face. Was he wiping the tears from his eyes . . . or laughing at me? Then the towel came down, and Papa seemed to be turning something over in his mind.

He said thoughtfully, "Ah, but Mama does change, and she does accept new ways when she sees good reason. It's against all custom, yet she's happy to have Zoe say the *Pistevo* in church to-morrow."

"What are you talking about? Zoe's not *really* going to say it. That's a joke, isn't it, Papa?" I asked.

"No, *Zaharia*," Mama stood in the doorway with her hands on her hips. "You altar boys are the joke, says Father Kouras. A bad joke, to read from the book instead of reciting the *Pistevo*. Well, he won't have it that way while the bishop is here for the holiday."

It's true the priest has been after us all to memorize the Creed. But as I said, the words in it are jaw-breakers. Nobody trusts himself without the book, not even Tom Thomas, who's fifteen.

Tears streamed down my face like Niagara Falls. Those onions were getting to me, too. The mental picture of being replaced by a peanut-sized six-year-old who happens to be my one and only sister made me shudder through my tears.

"I'll never be able to look my friends in the eye if Zoe does that," I objected. "I won't let her, I won't."

"It's not for you to decide," Mama answered firmly.

"You never trust me to decide anything. Never!"

"Did not you and the other boys decide by ignoring Father's wish that you memorize the prayer?" Papa said. "You have no quarrel with Zoe. She's simply doing what she's been told to do."

"You think Zoe's so good. Well, the only thing

she's good at is making me look bad. I wish . . . I wish I was born to a family that's lived in America since 1492," I yelled. I left the store with Mama's voice calling, *"Zaharia*, don't forget to take a bath tonight. . . ."

If I could think of somewhere to go, I'd stay out all night. Instead, I sat on the curb of the little park under the streetlight while Mama took Zoe home and got her to bed. If Zoe's so big, she ought to stay by herself in the house. But I don't get any choice in that, either. So, as usual, after Mama headed back to the store, I went slowly upstairs.

Although she was supposed to be sleeping, Zoe came and banged on the door of the bathroom, where I had locked myself in. "Zach, you're not under the water, are you? I have to come in."

"Hold your horses and wait until I'm good and ready to come out," I said to keep her from busting in.

"I don't need the toilet," said Zoe. "I need to talk to you. I know the whole *Pistevo*, I think, Zach, but if I get stuck, you gotta help me."

"I don't 'gotta' anything, Zoe," I said.

"Yes, you do, Zachary Athanasius Poulos, 'cause that's your job. To help me. You always do."

"God helps those who help themselves," I told her through the closed door and stuck out my tongue. It made me feel better even if she couldn't see it.

That wasn't the end of her pestering. She insisted

121

on practicing the prayer out loud in the dark from her bed. Lying in my bed I could hear her like some windup toy going through it over and over. Fourth or fifth time through, she tripped on the part about the Holy Spirit, the Lord, the Giver of Life. It stopped her cold.

"I lost the picture," she wailed.

It sounded wacky, but I knew what she meant. We both learn the same way. When I study something on a page, the whole page stays in my head. If I'm trying to remember an answer for a quiz, I call up a picture of the page in my head and look at it until I find what I need.

I had been doing exactly that as Zoe recited, so automatically I fed her the next words: " . . . *to ek too Patros* . . ." Then I realized what I'd done. Only an idiot would help Zoe with the job of making himself and the other altar boys the laughingstock of the whole city.

The next morning Tom Thomas was a step ahead of me and my thinking. He and two other altar boys were waiting outside our door when we came down, ready for church. I could tell he'd heard.

"If altar boys are not good enough to say the Creed, then we can't be good enough to do the rest of the service, right? You agree?" Thomas asked, glaring at me.

"What d'ya mean?" I asked uneasily. "I agree it's a mess. But what can we do about it?"

"We can go on strike, that's what. The minute Zoe steps up from the front row, we all walk off of the altar, sit down in the front row, and fold our arms."

I had to clear my throat before asking, "You mean, we don't serve from that moment on? How's the priest going to give communion and who's going to hold the candles? He won't be able to finish."

"You got the message all right, Zach, and so will the bishop and everybody else in church," he announced grimly. "Furthermore, since the baby replacing us happens to be *your* sister, you're going to be the one to lead us out."

"But . . ."

Tom Thomas didn't let me finsih. "The only 'but' about this, Zach, is the sore butt that someone will have if he doesn't join the strike."

"Sore butt *and* a sore head," said one of the other guys. "You and Miss Priss better think it over."

Then all three turned and marched rapidly away down Central Avenue.

Zoe grabbed my hand and yelled at their backs, "My Zach thinks better than you or anybody, 'n' I'm no baby." Tugging me along, she said, "We're gonna be late. Zach, what's a strike? Will it hurt us?"

What a question. I groaned. Go on strike and the priest, the bishop, Mama, Papa—everybody— would be down on me. Who knows? The church roof might even cave in. Let Zoe recite, and the guys would be waiting in the alley to come down on me. The four-and-a-half block walk to the church felt like the condemned man's last mile to me.

Even Zoe had gotten the message, because she fell silent. At the church door she let go of my hand finally and asked, "Zach, maybe we should pray for an early 'amen'?"

"No hope of that, Zoe. Not with a bishop here, and it's a holy day besides. Better pray for something like a miracle."

We lit our candles and put them in the box of sand by the icon. After we crossed ourselves, Zoe whispered, "You said God helps those who help themselves, so we're okay, 'cause I prayed for God to help you take care of everything . . . *zap*, just like that."

Don't I wish I could believe in Santa Claus and miracles the way Zoe does. I left her sitting in the front row and went through the door to the altar. Putting on my blue-and-gold robe, I noticed that the skirt came only to the top of my ankles. Lucy was right. I've been growing faster since my tonsils came out. But not fast enough, my mind added gloomily, since Tom Thomas and the others are all much bigger.

Halfway through the service I sneaked a look out into the church. On the bishop's throne at the front of the church, the bishop sat with both hands around his staff and his eyes closed. Probably to keep the sight of all us sinners from muddying his eyes. Zoe, her eyes fixed firmly on the Eye of God painted over the altar doorway, was nervously moving her lips.

My mind was a blank. No thoughts, only pictures kept popping into my head: Zoe under the maple tree scrunching her eyes shut to recite, Tom Thomas glaring, me in bed feeding Zoe the words she needed.

The deacon was singing, "The doors, the doors, in wisdom let us attend."

I stiffened. Only seconds now to go before Zoe had to step forward. Tom Thomas sent a meaning-filled look across the altar at me. I glared back. One word came into my head: escape.

The priest, who had raised the cloth to shake it in the air, repeated what the deacon had said and waited. We all waited. Not a sound broke the silence. Out of the corner of my eye, I saw Zoe, who had stepped forward, standing very still. Her mouth was simply opening and closing like a fish gulping for air.

That's when I did it. I turned and bolted out the altar door. Galloping faster than Whirlaway in the Kentucky Derby, I made it to the step in front of the altar before the other altar boys could move. Zoe grabbed my hand and sagged against me.

I shoved her back upright with my leg and started loudly: *"Pistevo eis enan theo . . ."*

With the picture of the page in my mind's eye, I moved steadily onward. Before the end of the first paragraph, Zoe's voice, squeaking, had joined mine. We finished reciting together, and the bishop beckoned us to his throne. I tugged Zoe forward, and she, copying me, bent and kissed his hand.

I let out my breath in relief one minute too soon. Just as we turned back to the center of the church, Zoe, in plain view of the whole church, picked up *my* hand and kissed it! Like a giant wave, smothered laughter rippled through the whole church from front to back. Even the priest was grinning when I took my place again at the side of the altar. I do wish Zoe would be little more private about how she feels.

Tom Thomas thought we had planned it all ahead of time. I didn't see any reason to tell him otherwise. Every time a lady friend came up to Mama outside of church to congratulate her for having such smart, good kids, Mama puffed up a little more. On the way home I swore she was going to float away like a balloon. She was calling Papa to come listen to her news before she even opened the screen door.

"And, Papa, clever Zach, who knew the *Pistevo* all along, stepped forward so quick, no one guessed our Zoe was dumb with fright at first," Mama said, chuckling.

"I've noticed, as you must have noticed, that our Zach . . ." Papa paused in the middle of his speech. Then he said with careful emphasis, *"Our Zach can be trusted to keep a cool head and do a good job, yes?"*

"Yes, Papa. You're right." Mama spoke soberly, but she didn't stay that way. Chuckling again, she said, "To think it was our Zachary and Zoe. The *first* time a girl says it, the *first* time that a brother and sister together . . . and in front of the bishop himself."

"That's America for you," Papa answered. "It just shows that to be Greek American is a new and different life, with new customs."

"Ah, yes," said Mama with a big sigh of satisfaction. "Only in America could this be. In fact, Papa, the priest and bishop say maybe soon they will have the prayer said in English, too." Mama looked over at me and said sharply, "Naturally, those who know it already in Greek should be the *first* to learn the English."

Papa was hunting in the back of the cash register drawer for something. He said, "A simple enough task for our Zachary, although he earned honor enough for us today. Did the priest say anything about the laborer being worthy of his hire?"

Mama looked puzzled, and Papa went on. "Seems to me, those who memorized so well deserve to be rewarded." He held up the two pieces of cardboard that he had finally found. "I have these two tickets for the boat ride Monday. Pity to let them be wasted."

The silence that followed was more awful than when I was waiting for Zoe to recite. Head cocked, Mama plainly was thinking.

At last she spoke. "But those tickets will not be wasted for Zach and Zoe will use them. Zach knows well how to keep an eye on Zoe, and both will learn from the trip and the teacher." Then her mouth curled up in a smile, her voice got all soft and dreamy. "Oh, Papa, I wish you could have heard *Zaharia's* voice . . . his pronunciation, so clear . . . Some day, perhaps we may even hear him speaking from the bishop's throne."

"Who knows what the future will bring?" Papa answered solemnly, but looking over at me he winked.

Boy, only a mother could have thought that one up. The idea of me growing up to become a bishop was enough to make a dead man laugh. Having Zoe included in my reward was no laughing matter, of course, but right now I had something bigger to worry about. What do people wear on a boat trip?

6
The All-Americans Score

"I'm squish-squashed, Zach," Zoe wailed. "Worse than the pea under the princess's twenty mattresses."

I barely heard her, and nobody could see her. Everybody and his cousin—a thousand people, I bet—had lined up to board the *Robert Fulton*, and we were smack in the middle of the crowd.

"Put your elbows out to make more room for yourself," Patty advised. She stuck out her own arm and for the hundredth time patted the bangs in her new haircut. She was all spiffed up in a blue top and pants that matched.

I looked down at Zoe. Her grip on my pants leg was tighter than an octopus's hold on his dinner. I said, "Whatever you do, don't pull or you'll yank my pants right off."

Both my pants and shirt were new. I had told Mama Americans don't wear Sunday church clothes on a picnic, they wear what's called casual clothes. *Amazingly, Mama had listened.* After checking with Mr. Cohen in the clothing store up the block, she bought me tan cotton slacks and a navy polo shirt for the picnic.

The crowd, which had started rolling up the gangplank, carried us along. We hardly had to move our feet. Just at the top Patty wobbled. It looked like she was going to pass out on the spot. If she did, she'd be steamrollered flat by the gorilla-sized guy right behind her. Abe moved in quickly. He butted the guy back, and Patty landed straight up and safely on deck.

"Whew," said Patty. "I couldn't breathe and my head started to spin. Am I glad you were right there, Abe."

"Anytime for a Musketeer," Abe said.

Then—of all the dumb things to do, the two of them just stood looking at each other. "What are you two staring bug-eyed at?" I said. "Let's find a safe place to stow our stuff."

Piling sweaters on a couple of steamer chairs and the rest of our gear underneath, we moved to the rail. Zoe's head came just even with the top of the rail, but she mashed her nose against the screen fence and looked through that.

Everybody itched to explore, but nobody could agree on where to start. Tiny wanted to work down from the top of the boat, while Louie argued for beginning with the engine room.

"There's plenty of time to see all of it, and we can

split up to do it. The top deck by the head shed is our home base." I pointed toward the pilothouse up top.

Right away I spotted the captain. He wore a snappy white cap and a brass-buttoned coat with four gold stripes on the sleeves. Unbuttoning his coat, the captain pulled out a gold watch, as big as a turnip, from his vest pocket. He snapped open the case, nodded, then raised and lowered his left hand in a signal.

Mbooo. The steam whistle blast made me almost jump out of my skin. Suddenly I felt a powerful throbbing come up through the soles of my feet. The boat was pulling away from the dock.

"Hallelujah and amen!" I yelled, and laughed. Up to that last moment, I had worried that something would happen to keep us from making the trip.

"Anchors a-way, my boys, anchors a-way, Abe sang.

"Your voice is enough to scare little children," Tiny told him. "Besides, wrong tune, Abe. Listen."

Tiny was right. Abe sounded like a sick Donald Duck, and somewhere on the boat a real live band was playing "God Bless America."

"Let's go find the music, guys," said Patty, bright blue eyes sparkling.

To my surprise, Abe said, "I'm going with Patty."

Zoe, who had been sticking to me like glue, asked excitedly, "I c'n go anywhere at all?"

"Anywhere, everywhere, Zoe, except . . ." She

scowled at me. I laughed out loud, then said, ". . . except *overboard*."

"I'm a explorer, and I'm goin' by my own self," Zoe announced. "Look, there's my friend Gina." She waved and snaked away through the crowd.

I yelled after her, "Don't forget where home base is."

Boy, the river was wide. Out in the middle of it, I could see how Henry Hudson mistook it for the passage to the Indies.

"Hey, Zach, guess what I found? This thing has a snack bar," said Tiny, who came up behind me.

Louie rushed up, screeching, "C'mon up front, Zach. The bridge is up, the bridge is up."

The *Robert Fulton* is so big, the Dunn Memorial Bridge has to be raised for the boat to pass. We all raced forward and wiggled our way up to the bow. The whole center section of the bridge had been lifted up and we were passing between the towers holding the cables that hoist the bridge.

"Aren't we hot stuff! Look at how everybody has to wait for us," I said. On both sides of the river gates held back growing lines of cars.

"How did they know to get the bridge up in time for us?" Mousie marveled, his nose twitching a mile a minute.

"Bud Fenner says the three whistle blasts while we're boarding warns the guy in the tower to start clearing the bridge of traffic. Then the single blast tells him we're on our way out, so he knows to start lifting the bridge. Where's Abe?" I wondered. "He likes to see things like this."

"Oh, he set up his chess set in the music lounge. I think he's gonna teach Patty how to play."

"Funny, I never heard Patty say she wanted to learn," I said, shaking my head. Today was an unusual day in every way, I guess. "Bud said to be sure to look at the walking beam. Coming with me?"

Louie, who left us to find some Elm Street friends, missed a good show. That walking beam, tipping up and down on the top deck like a giant teeter-totter, was something to see. A guy could get hypnotized watching.

Henry from Armory Garage explained to me that steam is what makes everything move. And the walking beam sends that motion down through shafts and cranks to turn the paddle wheels, which are what pull the boat through the water. Between what Henry told me and some questions that I asked Bud Fenner, I got a fair idea how it all works. But nothing beats seeing it in action for yourself.

Finding the part that pushes the wheels was easy. On the bottom deck we came across this large brass cylinder running smack through the middle of the boat. The brass-cased shaft, about waist-high on an adult, actually blocked the passage. Grown-ups who tugged little kids away plainly thought the setup was a pain in the neck. Maybe, dangerous. But the revolving cylinder that enclosed the shaft was so big and shiny nobody could could bump into it by accident. The only way around was to go upstairs and come back down on the other side of the shaft.

A bunch of people, including Zoe and her friends, stood watching it turn. When she noticed us, Zoe said, "Zach, it's a game. This guy here double-dared 'em to ride on it, and he's going first."

To me, it looked harder than riding a bucking bronco. That polished brass had to be as slippery as ice and turning constantly, it was bound to throw him off.

"My uncle told me he used to do it," Mousie muttered. "The trick is to let go in time to land on your feet and not on your head."

Tiny whispered in my ear, "This crowd is from the North End. They're pretty tough guys."

A beefy kid, who looked to be sixteen, moved up closer to the shaft, eyed it for a second, and leaped up to belly-flop on it. At the last minute he lost his nerve and let go. He slid back and hit the deck with a thump.

He looked comical sitting on his bottom, and we laughed.

One of the other big kids said, "Think you can do better?"

Zoe piped up. "Sure. It's easy."

"So, we're waiting. Show us how," a redhead with freckles said, ignoring Zoe to look directly at me.

What a talent Zoe has for opening her mouth and putting *my* foot in it! Mousie and Tiny had bunched up close to me. I forced myself to take a step forward.

Then Zoe shouted, "Me first," and darted ahead of me.

"Get outta the way, ya little shrimp," growled the beefy guy.

"I called first, so I get to go first," she insisted. "an' I'm no shrimp. I'm a people." Arms raised, Zoe looked like a swimmer at the beginning of a stroke. She said, "One . . . for the money, two . . . for the show . . . three to get ready . . ."

"What you are is a real killer-diller," said the redhead. He pretended to duck away in fright.

The whole crowd from the North End was laughing so loudly now that it was hard to hear the count clearly. "Four . . . to go," came before I could open my mouth to order her back.

Zoe jumped up in the air and forward. It worked. Skinny arms hugged the top of the crankshaft, and her body hung itself on the case. The turning shaft was carrying her up like some limp wet rag that got draped on it.

"Zach, peel her off before she gets hurt," cried Tiny.

"I can't stand to watch," moaned Mousie.

Though my brain was working double-time on where Zoe might land, my feet felt like I was wearing cement shoes. No way could I reach the other side in time to catch her if she got tossed off. I dropped to the floor anyway. My idea, crazy but the only one I had, was to crawl under the shaft and try to cushion her fall.

It takes longer to tell than Zoe's whole trip did. Toes planted now on the case, her feet inched toward her chin. Her rear end stuck straight up in the air. She reminded me of an inchworm as she pulled into a crouch at the top of the shaft's turn. Then Zoe shot off the case, somersaulting once, and landed, light as a cat, on her feet on the other side.

"Holy Toledo . . ." "Look at her go . . ."

"Didn't I say it was easy?" a beaming Zoe called back over the barrier of the crankshaft.

The gang of big kids wasn't laughing now, but Tiny and Mousie were. They waved at Zoe and told her to come back. Squatting, she duck-walked back under the shaft.

"I never saw anybody move so fast. She double-jointed or something?" asked a freckle-faced kid.

Zoe cocked her head and said, "I been practicing my tumbles for our 'lympics." Turning to me, she asked, "Am I what he said, Zach?"

"Double-jointed? No, it's the practice, Zoe."

"We all been practicing to be 'lympics champeens," Zoe announced to the big guys. Still grinning, she turned to look at the boy with Gina. "Wanna see me do a double tumble off the top?"

"I don't believe her garbage about Olympics and

practicing. That was just a freaky piece of luck," said the beefy guy. He gave me a dirty look. "Let's see Mr. Wise Guy here try it."

I swallowed. I sure haven't been somersaulting around town like Zoe. But would I look like a baby if I didn't try? Or would he listen if I explained that my special event was swimming and diving?

Okay, let's face it, I'm truly champion only of the speedy talker event. And right now I needed to win the speedy thinker one, too. Did some general say that the best defense is an offense?

I launched a counterattack. "One for one. Our side has a winner. You guys try again, and then I'll lead the next round."

Tiny, supporting me, said, "That's a fair enough offer."

I studied their faces for a clue as to what would come next. Having to look up at guys taller and bigger didn't help, but I tried to look cool as a cucumber.

"Move along, kids. This is no place for playing games." The deep voice took us all by surprise. Behind us was a ship's officer. He pointed his thumb at the stairs and added, "Upstairs, and don't try to ride the shaft on the other side of the boat, either, because somebody is keeping watch there."

I stepped back to let the North Enders go first. "Can't say I'm disappointed," I murmured to Tiny. After such a close shave with that crowd, I got a sudden urge to find all our friends. "Anybody see Louie? Let's check out Abe and Patty."

In the lounge, people were dancing to "When You Wish upon a Star."

"Get a load of that couple," Mousie snickered, nudging me to look.

A pea-sized diamond ring on the man's pinky finger caught my eye first, then the shiny lavender shirt and wavy golden hair. The lady whose dark hair hung loose in a cloud wore a fluttery flowered dress. Steve the Pigman and Lucy the Icelady were plastered together like wallpaper on the wall and swaying to the music. I wasn't surprised, but I felt kind of sorry that Steve could go so sappy over a girl.

"Look in the corner," Tiny said, pointing. "Isn't that Abe playing chess?"

We skirted the edge of the dance floor and came up to where Abe sat hunched over a chess set on a coffee table. Patty perched on the arm of Abe's chair. A bearded man sitting opposite studied the board.

"Abe, you want to . . ." I started to ask.

"Sssh," Patty whispered."That man said Abe has the makings of a champion, and he should know because he's a biggie in chess tournaments."

Abe gave Patty a sidelong look. With a smarmy smile, she reached out and gave his shoulder a little squeeze. I know the Musketeers are all for one, but the way Patty was behaving was ridiculous. I opened my mouth to tell her so when I saw Abe reach up, almost absentmindedly, for her hand.

Abe Pincus Zalkin and Patricia Zelda Aylward were holding hands. If I'd been kicked by a mule, I couldn't be more stunned.

"Good heavens, young man, you may have trapped me," said the bearded man.

Patty's blue eyes blazed with pride. Feeling like the fifth wheel on a wagon, I turned abruptly and left. On deck I took a deep breath of fresh air to steady myself. I decided to work my way through to the front of the crowd around Miss Lang. Once again Zoe was there before me. She had her friends with her, too.

"Today we speak English here. *But*," said Miss Lang, loud and clear, "many of the first European settlers in the Hudson Valley came from the Low Countries." She turned and spread-eagled her fingers across part of a world map taped to a wall. "Dutch from Holland, Walloons from Belgium."

Zoe raised her hand as if in class and cut in with a question. "I don't understand. Why do you call them the Low Countries when they're so high up on the map?"

All around us people were chuckling and laughing. Zoe hasn't read *Hans Brinker* yet, so she doesn't know about the Netherlands being so flat and below sea level even. I had some questions of my own like:

What do Walloons speak? Walloonese? But after Zoe's boo-boo, I sure wasn't going to ask Miss Lang.

The laughs from the crowd didn't slow Zoe down. She sailed on. "What's that place on shore? What are those boats doing?"

Miss Lang smiled approvingly. "I'm glad you asked. Brickyards where they make and bake bricks have existed along our river from Colonial times. The barges being loaded will take bricks to New York City just as they did one hundred years ago."

I wasn't in the mood for a history lesson, but Lang did make the shore more interesting to look at. Zoe drew in a breath—to ask another question, I'm sure, but just then the *Fulton* gave a blast on its whistle. From the brickyard on shore came an answering blast from another steam whistle. Passengers cheered and waved at two kids on shore who were flapping a big white sheet at the boat.

"They're signaling," I said, stopping Zoe's unspoken question. "Maybe the captain is a friend. Let's go to the other side to watch the boat dock at Hudson."

"Gina and Peter, you come, too. Ouch. Don't do that or I'll bop you, Peter." Peter promptly tugged Zoe's pigtail again, but she only giggled.

At the city of Hudson, people were lined up to board the boat just the way we did at Albany. Kids' voices shouted, "Here, over here," and I saw two heads bobbing in the water. A man next to me at the rail pulled back his arm and tossed a penny into the air. Like sharks going after a meal, the heads in the water raced toward where it would drop. From the top deck a whole shower of pennies rained down, and more kids jumped into the river to catch the pennies.

"I bet Zach could catch more pennies than anybody," said Gina.

"I'd rather be the person who has extra pennies to throw away," I answered.

"Gina likes . . . I know who Gina likes. . . ." Zoe sang and danced around Gina, who blushed fiercely.

That was my cue to leave I decided, and I headed for the engine room to find Louie. Windows opening onto the machines let passengers see the engineer work the levers. Louie must have been and gone already, but I stood around a while, watching.

Best of all was the oiler. Holding onto a grab bar and leaning out over an engine, he gave a handle a half-turn. If he had had long sleeves on and if a sleeve got caught, his arm would be minced meat. Since nothing as exciting as that was happening, I left.

While the boat was docking at Catskill, I ran into Tiny and Mousie at the rail. "You guys see Louie the Lip?" They shook their heads no, and I sort of answered my own question. "It's a boat, so he can't get lost or be very far from us."

We had steamed down the river almost to Kingston before I found Louie. And then I didn't know I'd found him because my mind was totally taken up with someone else.

A group of girls, sunbathing by the walking beam, shrieked and giggled, the way girls do when they want you to pay attention to them. I wasn't going to do them that favor, so I started moving past at a good clip.

Clip is the right word, too, because of what happened to me next. I got clipped on the back of the head by something hard. Whirling, I saw the missile lying on the deck. Of all things, it was a small bottle.

A girl's tanned hand reached for it, but I got there first. You can't hit a girl back, but I could make sure she didn't get a second chance with the bottle. Not having any trust in girls, I raised my arm to throw it overboard.

"Keep-away, he wants to play keep-away," someone shouted.

The girl reaching out straightened to look me in the eye, and my brain went numb. Even though I hadn't seen the face before, I knew who she was instantly. Hair the color of clover honey waved and curled down below her shoulders. It was the girl from Lincoln pool, and I blurted out, "Honey!"

"Oh, I didn't know you cared!" said the honey-colored girl, laughing and showing snow-white teeth.

I noticed, too, she had a tiny mole or beauty mark at the corner of her right eye. Looking at that, I couldn't help paying attention to her eyes as well. They were a deep chocolate brown and had a curtain of thick, sooty eyelashes.

"I m-mean I thought . . . uh . . . the bottle . . . uh had honey in it."

A girl shouted, "Hey, Dessie, you lost the contest. Louie is the champion."

This pain, hard but sweet, stabbed me somewhere in my chest and then, like a dagger made of sugar, it melted. What kind of name was Dessie or Tessie? And what did Louie win?

Dessie put her hand out. "Can I have my lotion back? Somebody else may want to try."

I saw Louie then. Surrounded by girls, he was juggling a golf ball, an orange, and a packet of crackers. Louie never told me he could juggle. And why didn't he tell me that his Elm Street friends were the girls from Lincoln Park?

"Do the seal-balancing act again," a girl urged him.

Louie obliged by tipping his head back and balancing the crackers on his nose. All the girls clapped and laughed as he staggered around in circles to keep the crackers from falling off.

"Terrific, Louie," Dessie called.

Big deal. Louie's got a nose like a ski jump. It's no surprise the crackers didn't fall off. Looking over the top of Dessie's head, I said, "I didn't know this boat had a zoo." I dropped the lotion bottle into Dessie's outstretched hand and began to walk away.

"Wait, why don't you try, too?" Dessie asked.

"I'm the zoo keeper. I don't play with the animals." I got inspired by my own snappy comeback and added, "It's almost feeding time, Louie. We land in a few minutes. If you don't come with me to collect your lunch, you'll be one hungry seal."

When we spread out our stuff on a picnic table in the park, those girls settled at the very next one. Louie, I noticed, sat at the end nearest to them. We'd finished eating, and I told myself not to look over at that Dessie. Naturally, my eyes immediately disobeyed. Worse, I got caught because in that same moment she looked at me.

"Anybody know where we put our garbage?" I asked, pretending to be looking in that direction for a trash barrel.

"Don't ask me," said Steve the Pigman, who was walking by with Lucy. "I'm on holiday."

Abe looked at me strangely. "You need glasses or something? The trash barrel is right here."

I was rattling my brain to find a way to change the subject when Zoe rushed up and saved me.

"He says he won, but I say he jumped the gun

and got a head start," she declared, pointing at Peter. "Zach, we need a starter and a finisher for our races."

"Some people we know say I don't see too well, Zoe."

"I'll be your starter, Zoe, if Steve will take the finish line," said Lucy. The way she smiled at him, I knew Steve would agree.

The little kids ran their race over, and Steve called it a tie between Zoe and Peter. Zoe took that as a win. She stuck her tongue out at Peter, who pulled her pigtails again.

After that we got some bigger kids' races going. Almost everybody in the park joined in. Naturally, Patty was one of the first up.

"Hey, that girl has gotta go. We can't race with girls," said a kid from the North End crowd.

"You afraid I'll beat you?" Patty challenged him.

I thought he was going to shove her out of the starting line. From the look on her face, so did Patty.

Lucy strolled up. She kind of stretched and flexed her arms, which made her muscles show. "This is a free country. She wants to race, she races. You don't want to race with girls, you don't race. You understand me?" she asked.

He understood all right. He walked away from the lineup. Patty won that race easily, and I tied with Abe for fourth place. Louie was way behind.

"All champions and winners, follow me," Steve said. "I'm treating to sodas."

That let me out. I flopped belly-down on top of the picnic table. Too bad I have to wait till next summer to win a swim race. Cradling my head on my arms, I fell into a half-trance. That girl Dessie's face floated by my mind's eye. Which reminded me again: Louie never said he knew her. Sneaky, that's what he was.

Like an echo from my head, Louie's voice sounded close by. ". . . Romano." Why was he saying his name? Louie's family has a telephone. Was he giving Dessie his name and phone number?

Squinting through half-opened eyes, I saw Louie talking to a couple of North Enders. Or rather, he was edging away and giving short answers. "Yeah, it's an Italian name. So what?"

"Not Italian. Dago, dummy, you're a dago," the beefy kid said.

I know for a fact, Louie is no dummy. He sight-reads music better than anybody and works out batting averages in his head.

"This kid is worse than that," said the redhead. "You know, the wops are partners with the Nazis."

Now this last sentence was a *true fact*. Italy is part of the Axis and fighting against the Allies. Last October when the Italians invaded Greece, I felt funny every time I saw Louie. I couldn't help wondering if maybe his uncle was shooting at my uncle.

Still, that didn't give these guys the right to call Louie ugly pick-a-fight names like dago and wop.

Louie opened his mouth, but closed it again without saying anything. He turned and moved swiftly to put the table between them and himself. Then he spoke. "That's the Italian government. It's nothing to do with me. I'm as American as you guys."

"Didn't you say your name is Italian? Make up your mind," said the beefy kid.

"I was born here. I'm an American," Louie repeated.

"He doesn't know what he is but we do. He's an enemy."

Zoe, who'd come back complete with a grape soda mustache, observed, "Those guys have mean little hearts. Zach, you should make them stop calling names. They're lots bigger than Louie."

She was right. These kids were aiming to use Louie as a punching bag mostly because they were sore losers. But, she forgot to mention that they were lots bigger than me, too.

"It's Louie's business, not mine, Zoe. Anyway, he's not even a Musketeer," I said in a low voice.

Before Zoe could argue, the beefy kid said, "All dagos or wops oughtta go back to where they came from."

I sat up abruptly. Anybody who could say that and not see where the remark led was a dumb dodo. These guys were such fatheads, I'd probably have to *explain* any insults or names that I called them. Instead, I pointed out, "This would be an awfully empty country if you did send everybody back. The only people who didn't come from someplace else are American Indians, so you don't belong here, either."

"Who are you to tell me where I belong, you dumb Polack?" The beefy guy was really steamed up now.

"You got it wrong again. I'm a Greek *American*, Louie's an Italian *American*. Everybody I know is American *plus* something, which means we got more to offer."

"Pizza."

Dead silence. You could have heard an ant crawl as we tried to figure that one out.

"Pizza is Italian, that's all. I'm not offering any," added Louie hastily with a weak grin.

I tried to smother my laugh, but it came out anyway.

"You'll laugh outta the back side of your head when we finish with you," the redhead promised.

I didn't know if he meant Louie or me. I know what I hoped, of course.

"When I get done with you, you'll be the right size and shape for flushing down the toilet," said the beefy kid. He spoke very softly, which made him scarier yet. His eyes flickered to my side, where Abe had appeared. "I'll start with the wise guy first, then do the meatball and the kike. Gonna clean all you foreigners out of the country."

Was I scared? Any normal kid would be scared, and let me tell you, I'm as normal as they come. I couldn't help myself though. I still went right ahead and said, "You and the Nazis. That's how they started."

Whispering sounds and gasps told me we had an audience. Murmurs of "fight, fight" swept through a crowd that was growing bigger. I didn't need to hear them to know what was coming but I couldn't see any way to retreat.

I continued, "Today you're picking on what you call foreigners, tomorrow it's everybody who wears eyeglasses or anybody different from you. That's Nazi talk."

"I'm gonna make you eat your words. Take your pick: fists or wrestling?" was his answer.

"Neither one is fair. You're a lot taller and must weigh half again as much as Zach," said Steve, who'd come up behind me.

"That's okay. I'm willing. Whatever . . ." I shrugged and didn't say any more. I was afraid my voice would shake. I tried to keep my mind focused on a picture in my head: John Talbot's arms slicing cleanly through the water as he swam to the raft. I still had to answer John's letter when—or if—I got home.

Fights must be as contagious as whooping cough, because the whole crowd started arguing about whether it should be fists or wrestling.

"I know," Abe shouted. "Arms. It should be the American way . . . with arms."

I couldn't believe this was *my* friend talking. Don't arms mean pistols and rifles? Was Abe crazy?

Hands waving, Abe explained. "Arm wrestling. Indians arm wrestle. And they'll be sitting down, so it's more even."

I nodded with relief. Only my arm would get broken instead of my head and all the other parts of my body.

In seconds Steve had the crowd pushed back from the picnic table. He announced in a stern voice, "Two out of three pinnings wins. And no bad blood afterward. You shake hands and call it quits."

Sweat popped out in a wide band on my forehead. I wiped the palm of my hand dry, braced my elbow on the table, and gripped hands with the beefy kid.

Push, push, push. Like a locomotive picking up speed, the words repeated themselves in my head faster and faster. Mainly my idea was to keep him from flattening me too soon. Sweat rolled down my forehead. A fly landed on the end of my nose. I could feel my eyes crossing as I looked down at it. I needed a deep inhale to blow the fly off and I took it.

Bang! And our arms were flat on the table. The fly, dead, was underneath, I think.

"You did it! You zapped him good!" Zoe shrieked, bouncing up and down on the bench next to me.

Dazed, I saw that mine was the top arm.

The beefy kid snapped shut his mouth, which had fallen open. He grabbed my hand again, snarling, "Luck. Just luck."

But it wasn't. Or if it was, it was *his bad* luck. I won the second, and when he insisted on a third try, I won that. Shaking my hand, he mumbled something. I repeated his words, loud and clear, for everybody to hear, "The best man won, I guess."

"Hurray for Zachary Poulos, the one and only champion arm wrestler," Dessie shouted, jumping up and down like cheerleaders do.

Lucy slapped me on the back. "Aren't you glad your family makes you work in the store lifting all those cases of soda and stuff? Terrific way to build muscles."

Abe couldn't get over the outcome. He was still talking about it when we were going home on the *Alexander Hamilton*. "Boy, Zach, you even *smelled* angry, almost like a lit firecracker. You might say we had our Olympics—even my chess, after all. Need I add that you performed magnificently?"

Grinning, I replied, "Yes, you do need to say it."

"Consider it said, champ," answered Abe, bowing to me from the waist. "Are you coming up top?"

"Later," I promised.

I went to stand by myself in the stern and sort

through what had happened today. From early on when Abe had held hands with Patty to the end when I found I had muscles, this day was one big surprise. Some of my ideas have turned upside down.

In a way I've been worrying about mostly all the wrong things this summer. Size isn't everything. In fact, it isn't much of anything. Look at how that big guy flopped. Having the guts to take a risk and being willing to push yourself counts for more in the end than size. And John Talbot is a good guy to copy from.

Second, I'm going to stop worrying about what I should be when I grow up. Papa's favorite old Greek, a man named Plato, wrote: Know thyself. That's sort of what I did today. I'd learned something about what was inside Zach Poulos. If I do more of that, what to be when I grow up will come at the right time by itself.

Watching the twin wakes from the paddle wheels, I had another important idea. Dessie must have asked who I was because she had cheered me by name. That had to mean something.

Unfortunately, in the hustle of landing, I never found her to check out what it meant.

"Joe DiMaggio, the best baseball player in America," said Louie when I fell into step with him on our walk to the Plaza bus stop.

I said, "Okay, so DiMaggio is an Italian American

like you. More important, what's the last name of your friend Dessie, and where does she live?"

"Who knows? I just met up with those girls on the boat. You didn't ask her yourself?" said Louie.

"C'mon, Louie, don't hold out on me. Remember, we're all Americans together and besides, you owe me."

"Hang me in chains if I'm not telling the truth, Zach," Louie protested.

Horrified, I believed him. "Jeez, Louie, we'll never find her again. Not unless we hire a detective, and I don't have that kind of money."

"You need money, Zach?" asked Zoe. She jingled her pocket and pulled out two quarters. "You can borrow if you give it back double."

"Where did you get all that money, Zoe? Tell me the truth," I demanded. I had enough worries already. If Zoe was a thief . . .

"It's all mine. It's my marriage money," said Zoe smugly.

"What are you talking about?" I shook my head to clear it. One of us was crazy, and I knew it wasn't me.

"Peter gave it to me to marry him when we grow up. I didn't say yes yet. He's gonna ask his sister Dessie for more money and give it to me next time."

"Dessie is . . . ? What next time you talking about? What's Peter's last name?"

"Stop shouting, Zach. You're breaking my ears. Don't you know who they are?"

"Would I be asking you if I knew?"

"He's Peter Kanakis and his sister Dessie has a real name of Despina. 'Next time' is the St. Markos picnic Sunday, 'cause they're Greek American like us."

"Bingo!" I shouted and laughed.

"Now you know, does that make you glad?"

"Glad? Sure I'm glad," I said. "I'm glad Peter has a last name, I'm glad his sister has a real name. And I'm glad we're all alive and well and living in Albany, New York."

But I didn't tell Zoe what I was most glad about. Which is that Louie Romano is an Italian American. He'll be going to St. Anthony's picnic and not the St. Markos one.

7
Zoe's Own Book

My name is Zoe Poulos.

I live at 7 Central and 11 1/2 Central. 11 1/2 is my store. We sell hot dogs, hamburgers, and good pie.

I am in 2nd grade and like to read. My mama says I can write my own books when I grow up.

I have had birthdays for six years. My friend Bud says if I was a dog, I wood be forty years old. So I don't have to wait to write. I want to set down some of the things that happen to me when I was young.

I am a MusketEar which is a club for any who have inishals of Z.A.P. All of us Z.A.P.s went to picnick on a Greek man's farm. Thats Zachary (my brother), me (his sister), Abe (friend), Patty (friend).

Abe and Patty tied their legs together. (They are girlfrend-boyfrend now.) No body got to the finish line so no body won the 3 legged race. I told Dessie Zach wanted to tie with her. She made him come ask her himself.

We helped to cook. First you dig a hole and put

a fire in it. Then you put a whole big meat (lamb) on a stick over the fire. Papa gave the picnick two big, big jars of sauce for the hot dogs wich was for the kids to eat.

We hiked up a big hill and over the other side. Ice water comes out of the ground there. Its called a spring. The big kids took loads of spring water back to the men for washing dishes and coffee.

Greek coffee looks like mud on the bottom of each cup. One lady tells fortunes from the cup. You turn the cup upside down. But first you drink the coffee. The way the mud drys shows her the fortunes. They did not let kids drink coffee.

Peter K. (friend) gave me his soda and ten cents. I said Thank you and I did not say I like Louie better than him.

Zach and Abe took a turn to wash glasses when Mama told them. Some people leave glasses with stuff still in them. Zach said the wine would make the dishwater dirty. They did not want to do that or to make the grass dirty with wine so they drank up from all the glasses.

Work at a picnick is not like work at home. Zach and Abe laffed and laffed.

A man played a violin. We did dances, even the men and the ladees. You hold hands like in Ring Around A Rosy but not a ring that is closed. The ends are free. A leader pulls the whole line and does fancy steps. I did better than Zach or Abe. They tripped and fell down. Dessie got mad at them and told them to go away. Then they lay down in the grass and slept.

The man played Greek musick for singing, too. Greek songs sound like crying, but Papa, Mama, and all of them laughed at the end. No kids sang those songs, so Papa said give the kids a chanse to sing its their country. We sang three songs. I Been Working on the Railroad. My Country Tis of Thee. God Bless America. I saw men and Mama too cry. Then they all clapped for us kids. That's the story of the picnick.